Fish Facts & Bird Brains

Also by Helen Roney Sattler

Dinosaurs of North America
The Illustrated Dinosaur Dictionary
Nature's Weather Forecasters

ABCD
EFGH
IJKL

HELEN RONEY SATTLER

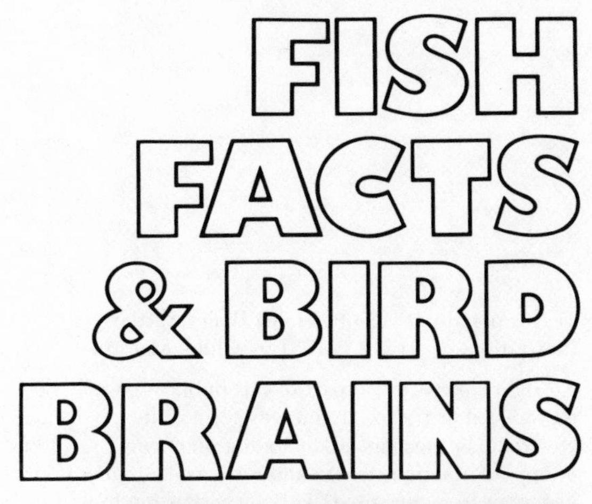

ANIMAL INTELLIGENCE

ILLUSTRATED BY GIULIO MAESTRO

LODESTAR BOOKS | E. P. DUTTON NEW YORK

Library of Congress Cataloging in Publication Data

Sattler, Helen Roney.
Fish facts & bird brains.

Summary: Discusses the intelligence of a variety of animals and the observations and tests which have brought scientists to their conclusions. Includes tests for the reader to use with pets.
1. Animal intelligence—Juvenile literature.
[1. Animal intelligence] I. Maestro, Giulio, ill.
II. Title.
QL785.S18 1984 591.51 83-20805
ISBN 0-525-66915-9

Published in the United States by E. P. Dutton
2 Park Avenue, New York, N.Y. 10016

Published simultaneously in Canada by
Fitzhenry & Whiteside Limited, Toronto

Editor: Virginia Buckley

Printed in U.S.A. W
10 9 8 7 6 5 4 3 2

dedicated to
Malinda

Acknowledgments

I especially want to express my appreciation and thanks to Biruté Galdikas, Jane Lancaster, William Lemmon, and Gary Shapiro for sharing their valuable time with me and answering my questions. I also want to thank the following authors, in addition to those in the Further Reading, for information gleaned from their scientific papers, articles, or books: Henry Blake, Elizabeth Borgese, Kent Britt, Robert Burgess, David and Melba Caldwell, Sally Carrighar, Robert L. Conly, Jacques Cousteau, Nicole Duplaix, Robert Epstein, Patricia Faul, Joyce Dudney Fleming, Karl von Frisch, Renee Fuller, Allen and Beatrice Gardner, Rick Gore, James Gould, R. W. Hingston, Winthrop Kellogg, Gerald Kooyman, Edward Linehan, Richard Lore, Walter and Margaret Luszki, William McElroy, Pamela McMahan, N. R. F. Maier, Daniel Mannix, Vance Packard, Maxine Rock, Duane Rumbaugh, Hope Ryden, E. Sue Savage-Rumbaugh, George Schaller, John Paul Scott, John Sparks, Shirley Strum, Adolph Suehsdorf, Claudia Thompson, Niko Tinbergen, Peter G. Viet, James Wiley, Guy Woodruff, and many others too numerous to mention.

I also extend appreciation and thanks to Mary Birkett for helping me locate reference materials and to Dorothy Kaiser French and Alice Thompson Gilbreath for reading and critiquing the manuscript.

Contents

1

Now That's Smart!

Dr. Wolfgang Koehler, a scientist, placed three wooden boxes of different sizes on the floor of his laboratory. Then he scattered sticks of different lengths around the room. Finally he hung a fragrant, ripe banana from the ceiling.

Into this room Dr. Koehler led a hungry young chimpanzee. Chimpanzees love bananas, but this banana was too high to be reached. Dr. Koehler left the chimp in the middle of the room and stood back to watch. He wanted to see how the chimpanzee would get the banana. Would it stack the boxes? Would it knock the banana down with a stick? Or would it give up and go hungry?

First the chimp sat on the floor and eyed the banana. It studied the boxes and the sticks. Then it looked at the scientist. The chimpanzee walked over to Dr. Koehler, grasped his hand, and led him to a spot beneath the banana. Then, using Dr. Koehler's body as a ladder, the clever chimp scrambled to his shoulders and grabbed the fruit!

The chimpanzee was smarter than the scientist had expected. It had thought of a solution the scientist had not.

Another scientist, Dr. O. A. Battista, put some candy on top of a stool. He placed the stool in the center of a tub of water on the kitchen floor of his summer cottage. Then he painted the edge of the tub with slow-drying glue. He wanted to find out if ants would be able to reach the candy. He knew that ants are clever. But he felt sure that he had outsmarted them. Ants could not get to the candy because they can't swim and they hate water. If the water didn't stop them, the glue would.

When Dr. Battista returned six days later, the candy was covered with ants. The ants had outsmarted the scientist. They had carried tiny pieces of grass and wood to the tub. Using saliva, they had glued the pieces together and built a bridge across the water to the stool.

Dr. Koehler and Dr. Battista were learning about the intelligence of animals. The doctors concluded that the chimpanzee and the ants were very intelligent, because they had understood their problems and had solved them in clever ways.

People once thought that animals were not intelligent. They believed that all animals acted by instinct—that is, they were born knowing how to do everything they needed to know in order to survive. They thought that only humans had intelligence. But people who had pets and those who worked with or trained animals did not agree. They knew that at least some animals could learn to do things they were not born knowing.

Then it was decided that only mammals could learn to work or do tricks. Some scientists wondered if this were so. They had seen ants and bees do some very clever things. They began to study different kinds of animals. Scientists watched wild animals in their own environment. They took animals to laboratories and tested them. By studying the intelligence of animals, they hoped to learn more about human intelligence and how humans learn. They also hoped that they could discover better ways of testing human intelligence and better ways to solve learning problems.

But what is meant by intelligence? People have different ideas of what the word *intelligence* means. They have been arguing about the meaning for a very long time. And they still do not agree. Some people think that intelligence is having a high IQ or making good grades in school.

If this were true, then animals, of course, could not be said to be intelligent. Intelligence is more than taking IQ tests or making good grades in school. A person may actually be very intelligent without making a high score on an IQ test. On the other hand, many people with high IQ's have done poorly in school.

Albert Einstein was one of the smartest men who ever lived, yet he did so poorly in school he was asked to leave. Thomas A. Edison's first-grade teacher told his mother he was too stupid to learn. He became one of America's greatest inventors.

No one knows everything. Einstein was a genius, but you may know something that he did not know. He flunked grammar and history. He flunked because he wouldn't study anything that did not interest him. Edison was weak in mathematics. But he was so determined and so dedicated that he earned patents on more than a thousand new inventions.

If intelligence is not making good grades, then what is it? Some scientists spend all their time studying the mind. They are called psychologists. Psychologists can't agree on just exactly what intelligence is, but they recognize it when they see it. They all agree that Dr. Koehler's chimpanzee and Dr. Battista's ants acted intelligently, in other words, behaved in ways that showed their intelligence.

Perhaps, then, we should look at actions instead of words to find the meaning of intelligence. Many psychologists claim that they can tell how intelligent people are by how they act or behave. When we think that someone is acting smart or stupid, we are recognizing behavior that is intelligent or not intelligent.

Intelligence is a combination of many traits, skills, and abilities. Some scientists believed that any animal that has a brain has some kind of intelligence. If an animal has any intelligence at all, it should be able to learn from experience, they decided. Therefore, they gave tests to many kinds of animals to see which ones could learn. They also wanted to find out how much each could learn. They discovered that some animals can learn better than others, just as some people can learn more than others. And some animals scored high on one kind of test and fairly low on another, just as a student may do well on a reading test, but not so well on an arithmetic test.

Start
Maze
End

2

Even a Worm Can Learn

Planarians are arrow-shaped, inch-long flatworms that live in ponds and freshwater streams. A scientist, Dr. William Corning, placed several planarians in an earthenware bowl filled with water. Then he turned on a bright light. After a couple of seconds, he gave the worms a mild electric shock. Planarians curl into a ball when they receive a very small electric shock. Dr. Corning wanted to see if he could train these planarians to curl up when only a light was turned on. Until Dr. Corning's experiment, most scientists didn't think that worms could learn anything because their brains are too tiny.

Dr. Corning was in for a big surprise! He discovered that planarians can learn very well. In only two days, his worms learned how to avoid a shock. When the light came on, the worms climbed out of the water and perched on the rim of the bowl. That was pretty clever for the lowest class of animals that have any kind of brain at all!

Another scientist taught planarians to run a maze. Flatworms may be the lowest animal that can learn. Starfish do not have a brain. Experiments with starfish show that they cannot learn to run even the simplest maze.

A maze is a wooden or plastic box with winding pathways. An animal learns to run the correct path in order to get a reward or to avoid a shock. Psychologists use mazes to test an animal's ability to learn and to remember. They say that learning is any change in behavior that is caused by experience. For example, you learn not to touch a hot stove if you get burned on one. You learn not to play with a sharp knife if you get cut with one. You learn even when making mistakes. Sometimes that is when you learn the best.

The way you learn shows how intelligent you are. The more you learn and the quicker you learn, the more intelligence you have. The quicker and better an animal can run a maze, the more intelligent it is believed to be.

Scientists test another kind of intelligence by trying to teach an animal to tell the difference between two shapes. In this test, if the animal presses a lever with the correct shape, it receives a reward of its favorite food. If it presses a lever with the wrong shape, it does not. The faster the animal learns which shape gives the reward, the more intelligent it is believed to be. Most mammals can do this rather quickly. But only a few invertebrates (animals without backbones) can learn it.

Although an octopus may not seem very bright, it quickly learns to run a maze for a tasty reward of crab meat. It easily learns the difference between a square, rectangle, triangle, and a circle, by sight. It can also be taught to pick out a cylinder of one size from a group of cylinders of another size by feeling them with its long tentacles. The octopus has a rather large brain and is more intelligent than most invertebrates.

However, insects are the most intelligent of the invertebrate animals. Insects learn to run mazes quicker and with fewer wrong turns than all other invertebrates. Cockroaches are fast learners and one kind of ant can learn to run a maze as quickly as a rat.

Not all animals can be taught to run mazes or to select shapes. Therefore, many scientists prefer to study and test an animal in its own environment. What an animal does naturally is a better test of its intelligence, these scientists believe.

For example, tumblebugs are beetles that lay eggs in dung, which will be used as food by the newly hatched young. The beetles shape the dung into a ball and transport it to the burrow by rolling it. They look rather silly rolling and tumbling over and over these balls of dung. But scientists have found that the beetles know what they are doing. If a rock or clump of grass blocks the way, the beetles study the problem. Then they either go around the rock or burrow under it. The grass may be chewed away. If the ball is squished flat or made into a square, the tumblebugs immediately mold it back into a ball. These beetles are able to solve problems and to tell the difference between shapes.

Dr. Niko Tinbergen, a famous Dutch scientist, spent many years studying the digger wasp—a wasp that eats only bees and

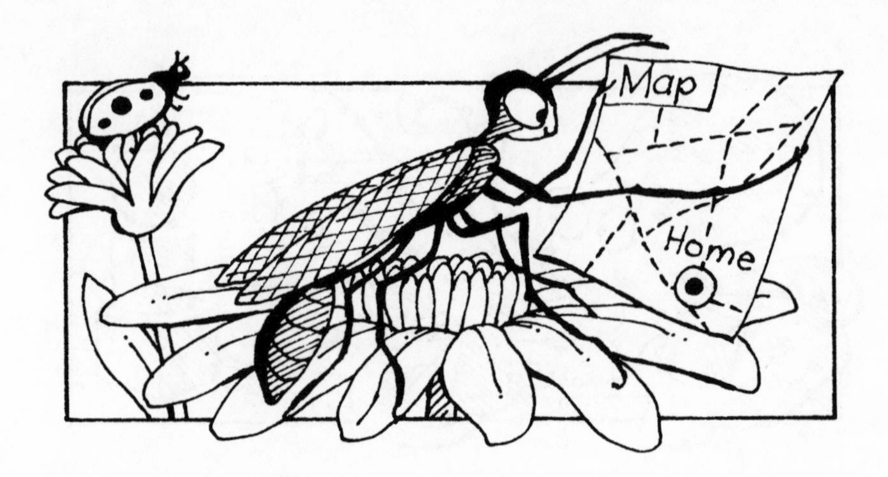

lives in a hole in the ground. Dr. Tinbergen wondered how such a small creature could find its own tiny hole among the many others close by. He noticed that when a wasp left its nest, it always circled over the burrow before flying away. He believed that the wasp learned the landmarks around its nest, and that was how it found its burrow when it returned.

To test this idea, he brushed away all rocks, sticks, and clumps of grass from around one nest, leaving only the burrow untouched. When the wasp returned, it flew to within four feet above its nest. Then it began darting back and forth, back and forth, searching for its nest. After a while, it landed and searched the ground. It took twenty-five minutes for the wasp to find its nest and stow its bee. Before flying off for another, it circled above the nest longer than usual. Then it returned and circled once again.

Another time, Dr. Tinbergen placed a circle of pinecones around a wasp's nest. When the wasp flew out, it circled over the nest several times before flying away. When it returned with its prey, it landed exactly in the center of the pinecone circle, then entered its burrow. Next Dr. Tinbergen moved the circle of pinecones a few feet away from the nest while the wasp was away. He carefully placed each cone as before. When the wasp returned, it flew to the center of the circle and began frantically looking for its nest. Only when Dr. Tinbergen moved the pinecones back around the nest did the wasp find it. This proved to the scientist that these wasps learned landmarks and needed only a few seconds to do it.

Of all the insects, honeybees are among the most clever. If you watch one honeybee move about from flower to flower, you will see that it always chooses the same type of flower. It pays no attention to other flowers in the same area. And it never goes to the same flower twice. It knows which flowers contain the nectar and pollen it wants. In order to do this, a bee has to have a good memory, an ability to learn, and be able to tell one flower from another.

Even more remarkable is the bee's ability to return to the hive once it has gathered its load. It may have flown hundreds of feet to find a suitable flower patch. But even on a cloudy day, it is able to make a straight line back to the hive. It must allow for any wind that might have blown it off its path. It must compute the sun's position, even on a cloudy day. And it must figure the distance the sun has moved to the west since it left the hive. (Bees, like many other animals, depend upon the sun to fix their locations.) This remarkable, tiny-brained insect can out-perform all but the very best human navigators even with their modern instruments.

Professor James Gould was fascinated by the bee's ability to judge the movement of the sun. He decided to try an experiment. He placed a dish containing a few drops of sugar water near the entrance of a beehive. After the bees had discovered it, he moved the dish farther away. Every few minutes, he moved the dish again. At first he moved it only an inch—then four inches, but each time he made the distance four times what it had been. Finally he moved the dish more than one hundred feet in a single jump. After a while, the bees "caught on" and were able to guess where the food would be the next time. They flew to that place and waited. Dr. Gould believes that bees use this same ability to judge the distance the sun moves.

What is more, honeybees have an elaborate dance language to communicate precise information to their hive mates. Using different movements, the scouts give the exact locations, the distance, the direction, and the size of new food sources. They also give detailed descriptions of possible new hive sites—the dryness, the size, the exposure to the sun, or any other important fact. By watching tagged bee scouts, scientists have learned that each scout checks out all the sites reported, and then all agree on the very best one.

Ants are probably even more intelligent than bees. A naturalist studying ants noticed that they never seem to use more helpers than are needed for one job. How do they do it? To find out, he cut a grasshopper into three sections. He made the second section twice as large as the first. The third was twice as large as the second. Then he gave the pieces to three different ant scouts from the same nest. The pieces were too large for a single scout to carry. Each scout studied its section and measured it with its antennae. Then the scouts went back to the nest for help.

The naturalist wondered—would each scout call out the same sized crew? Would an army of ants come back to the cut-up grasshopper and then divide up according to the number needed for each job? Would there be too few ants to carry the largest piece so that more would have to be sent for? Most animals learn by trial and error. They need to try several different solutions before finding the correct one. Would the ants have to do this?

The naturalist was surprised when he saw that the ant with the smallest grasshopper portion brought only twenty-eight workers. Forty-four came for the second, and eighty-nine for the third piece. Each ant had called out only the number of helpers needed to move its piece of grasshopper. The second brought nearly twice as many as the first, to move a piece twice

as large. The third brought almost twice as many as the second to move a piece twice as large. How could ants with their pin-head-size brains solve such a complicated problem? It took judgment to figure out the exact number of workers needed.

In another experiment, a tree limb containing the nest of leaf-cutting ants was placed in the middle of a large pan of water. The ants could not cross the water. But they could explore the branches of the limb. They soon discovered that one leaf stretched beyond the pan and was only two inches above the ground. The ants gathered on this leaf, their weight bending it still farther. Then one ant grabbed the edge of the leaf with its hind claws and hung down its full length. Another climbed down the first ant's body and held on to its head. Then a third and a fourth, until they had formed a chain to the ground. Now all the others escaped by climbing down this ladder of live ants.

Scientists have observed many such events in which ants changed their behavior to overcome a difficulty. They are the lowest class of animal known to be able to use several bits of information to solve problems. Of all the ants, the *Formica,* or common red ant, is the most intelligent. It is the genius of the insect world.

Another group of scientists found out that ants that eat a good diet during their growing stages learn better than those that eat a poor diet. Similar experiments with human children show that those who eat healthful, balanced diets rich in proteins and vitamins increase their ability to learn also. It may be possible to prevent many children from becoming slow learners.

Scientists have discovered many things from studying invertebrates. Invertebrates have good memories and can learn, tell the difference between shapes, communicate, solve problems, and use judgment. But vertebrates (animals with backbones) can do all that and much more.

3

Fish Facts and Bird Brains

Fish fascinated Dr. Konrad Lorenz, a world-famous naturalist, especially those that cared for their young. His office was lined with huge tanks of them. In one tank lived a family of jewel fish. Dr. Lorenz discovered that baby jewel fish follow their mothers the way chicks follow hens. At dusk, the mother put her babies to bed in a nest that the father hollowed out for them in one corner of the tank. The mother hovered over the nest and called her babies by rapidly flashing her brightly colored fins up and down. The young gathered under her and sank into the nesting hollow. Meanwhile, the father searched the tank for stragglers. When he found one, he sucked it into his mouth and blew it into the nest.

One day Dr. Lorenz fed the fish just as the mother was calling the young to the nest. He dropped some chopped earthworms into the tank. The mother refused to eat. However, the father grabbed a piece of worm too large for him to swallow. As he began to chew it, he saw a baby fish escape from the nest. He darted after the baby and sucked it into his already full mouth.

Now the fish had a problem! Dr. Lorenz wondered what would happen. He fully expected the father to swallow the baby along with the worm. Instead the fish stopped absolutely still. For many seconds he did not move, not even to chew.

"If ever I have seen a fish think, it was at that moment!" says Dr. Lorenz.

Finally the fish spat out both the worm and the baby. Both sank to the bottom of the tank. Then the father ate the worm. When he had finished, he sucked up the baby and carried it to the nest.

Dr. Lorenz was astonished. Here was a fish, the lowest form of vertebrate, with its tiny, primitive brain, deciding how to solve a problem. Scientists believe that it takes a special kind of intelligence to know how to care for the young. Dr. Lorenz's observations proved that this is true.

Experiments show that fish can learn to run mazes about as quickly as ants. Scientists at Pavlov Institute in Leningrad discovered that fish can also distinguish shapes. A container of food, equipped with a chute and a cord, was put on top of a goldfish aquarium. A pull on the cord caused food to fall into the water. The scientists tied a red button to the end of the cord. Then they taped a card with a circle on it to one end of the aquarium and dropped the button into the water. The fish immediately grabbed the button and swam off with it, yanking the cord. Food dropped into the tank.

The fish soon learned that whenever it pulled the cord, it got food. Then the scientists replaced the circle with a triangle. This time, when the fish pulled the cord, no food dropped into the tank. In a short time, the fish learned that it got food by pulling the cord when the circle was at the end of the tank, but not when the triangle was there. From then on, the fish pulled the string only when the circle was visible.

The scientists discovered something else. Like humans, some fish learn quickly, while others took much longer, and one fish learned better than all of the others. This wise fish learned to distinguish between twenty different pairs of designs.

Of all fish, sharks are the most intelligent. They learn about as well as rats, a much higher order of animal. Scientist Dr. Eugenie Clark wondered if sharks could remember. She did an experiment to find out. First, she taught a pair of lemon sharks to push a target that rang a bell. When they rang the bell, the sharks got a reward of food. They learned to do this quickly. In a very short time, they also learned to distinguish between a right and wrong target.

Then Dr. Clark stopped the experiments for two months. When the target was once again placed in the water, the sharks rang the bell to get food exactly as they had done before. Sharks can remember!

There are different kinds of learning. Mazes are solved by trial and error. With this kind of learning, you try one thing, and if it doesn't work, you try something else until you find the right solution. Sometimes it takes many attempts. Animals in the laboratory learn for a reward (a bite to eat), just as humans learn to do something for praise. Animals in their natural environment learn from experience and by association.

Amphibians, such as frogs and toads, are a little more advanced than fish. They learn to run mazes only a little better than fish, after many attempts. But in its natural environment, a toad learns very quickly. It may snap up a bumblebee once but never a second time. It learns in one lesson to avoid all fuzzy insects with a similar color pattern. It associates the color with the sting.

Reptiles learn a little better than amphibians. The king cobra is the most intelligent of the snakes. In captivity, a king cobra learns to recognize its keeper and, when hungry, lies by the feeding door and waits for him.

Crocodiles are probably the most intelligent of the reptiles.

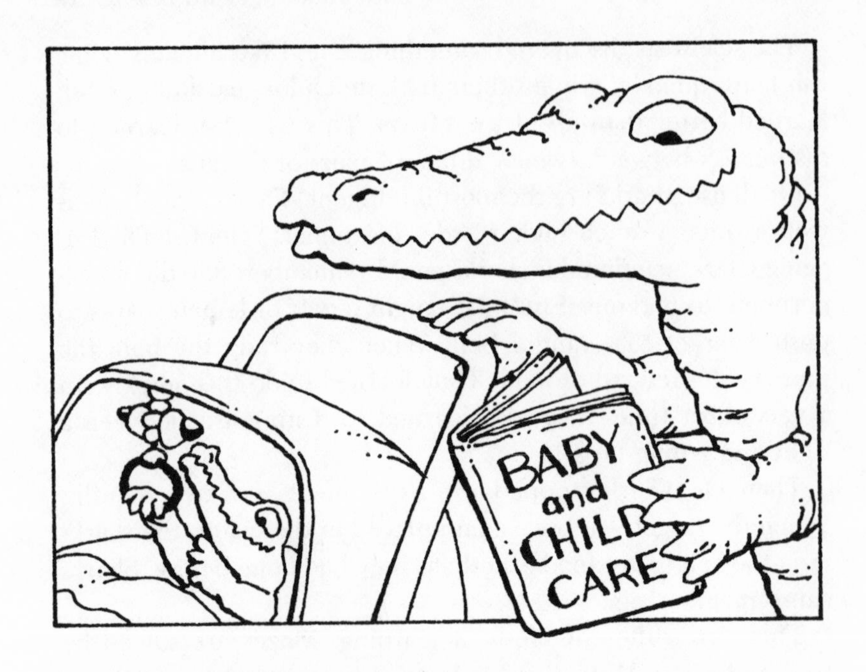

Their brains are far more developed than those of other reptiles. They learn quickly and are very good at adjusting their behavior to meet the needs of their environment. Some take care of their young, showing a mental ability seldom seen in animals lower than birds or mammals.

Birds are warm-blooded and belong to a higher order of animals than reptiles. They learn more rapidly and solve more difficult problems than the lower forms of vertebrates. Most birds do very well in laboratory tests. They quickly learn to peck the right lever to escape from a box and easily learn to tell the difference between shapes and colors. Pigeons have been taught to sort pills by color on a conveyor belt and to communicate with one another by means of symbols. A great spotted woodpecker learned to ask for any one of five different foods by using a simple telegraphic code.

In captivity, birds learn to do many kinds of tricks, including speaking words. Some crows and parrots even seem to use words in the right situations, saying "hello" when someone arrives and "good-bye" when someone leaves. One parrot at Purdue University learned to name forty different objects and to ask for them by name. It could identify four colors, tell the differences between shapes, and use the word *no* in the correct context.

The vocabulary of wild birds is even more amazing. Using vocal calls, postures, and motions, birds are capable of sending a great many messages. Crows give as many as fifty-six calls, ranging from distress calls to alarm calls and from assembly calls to attack calls. The herring gull uses sixty-three or more.

Just as human children learn to speak the language of their parents, young birds learn only the calls of their parents and not those of other birds nearby. Although the calls of the species are always the same, many birds are quite creative in their mating songs. They add variations to the songs sung by their parents.

It was once thought that only humans possessed the ability to communicate and to use tools. We now know that all birds communicate and several use tools. The Galapagos woodpecker-finch prods beetles out of crevices in dead trees with a cactus spine held in its beak. Egyptian vultures hold rocks in their beaks to crack open ostrich eggs. European song thrushes beat snails against rocks to break them open. Sea gulls drop clams, and blue jays drop nuts, onto rocks in order to break them open.

Bowerbirds actually make their own tools (a remarkable accomplishment for a bird!). These Australian birds make paintbrushes by pulling shreds from the inner bark of trees. For "paint," they crush berries or make a paste of saliva and chewed-up grass. These tools are used to decorate elaborate bowers that are built to attract a mate. Bowerbirds also decorate with fruits, flowers, feathers, shells, or any other colorful object that appeals to them. When a flower fades or a fruit shrivels, they discard it and replace it with a fresh one. Scientists claim that these birds are extraordinarily intelligent and talented.

Wild birds learn to avoid food that makes them ill. Most birds won't eat poisonous insects such as bees or wasps. An exception is the European bee eater, which has learned to get rid of the venom by holding the bee in its beak and rubbing the insect's abdomen on a limb or rock. Then it can safely eat the bee or give it to its young.

Possibly nothing demonstrates the shrewdness of a bird as well as its ability to escape capture. Most game birds are able to escape from a hawk, but some are shrewder than others. Pigeons try to stay above the hawk. If unsuccessful, a pigeon goes into a barrel roll, closing one wing and spinning out of reach. When attacked broadside, the bird folds its wings and drops like a shot. Zoologist Daniel Mannix once saw a crow shake a pursuing falcon by flying between two strands of barbed-wire fence. The falcon, having a wider wing span, was caught up in the wire.

Ground birds are just as clever at protecting their young. A mother quail, like most ground birds, darts from her nest and flutters a short distance ahead of a fox or other predator, dragging her wing as if it were broken. The predator immediately chases the apparently injured bird. When the bird has led the predator far from her nest, she flies off, returning to her nest only when the predator is gone. Scientists claim that this kind of behavior requires reasoning ability and awareness.

Some birds seem to be able to plan ahead. Woodpeckers, nuthatches, and blue jays store food for winter. Foresight—the ability to plan for the future—is considered an important part of intelligence.

The games that animals play show a great deal about their intelligence. Birds display great imagination in their games. Many play with objects such as twigs, moss, or stones. Others are more creative. A hummingbird was once observed playing in a stream of water from a garden hose. The bird landed in the water and let the water carry it to the end. It flew back many times and allowed itself to be carried down again. It seemed to be enjoying itself immensely.

Dr. Lorenz tells of observing jackdaws (European crows) playing with the wind during a storm in a similar fashion. These birds folded their wings and dropped like stones to tree-top level. There they spread their wings and allowed the wind to carry them aloft like kites. When they reached sufficient altitude, they turned themselves over, folded their wings, and dived like falling stones again. They did this again and again, sometimes soaring at eighty miles per hour. This required exact assessments of distances and the understanding of wind conditions such as crosscurrents and wind pockets.

Such behavior shows insight—the ability to see and understand the nature of something. Each bird saw an opportunity and took advantage of it.

Of all birds, the crow is considered to be the most intelligent. Without being taught, a wild crow knows the difference between a man carrying a gun and one carrying a stick or shovel. A person without a gun can get quite close to a wild crow. But a man with a gun cannot get within shooting distance of one, unless he uses a bird blind (a camouflaged screen).

It is hard to shoot a crow even from a blind, because a crow can count. If two men go into a blind and one leaves, most birds will resume feeding. But not crows. They know that another man is still there. They will resume feeding only after the second man leaves.

A laboratory experiment showed that a raven (a kind of crow) has a good concept of numbers up to seven. When shown a card with seven dots, the raven searched for seven pieces of food, but no more. When shown a card with five dots, it ate only five pieces of food.

Crows have remarkable memories, too. One flock remembered a man who had been seen holding a dead crow. They attacked and harassed that man every time they saw him.

Crows are well known for their curiosity, and there are many stories about remarkably clever ways in which crows have solved problems. A northern crow perched in a tree and watched fishermen catch fish through holes in the ice. It was too cold for the men to sit beside the lines, so they rigged them with red flags that popped up whenever a fish was caught. Before long, whenever the flag went up, the crow flew to the line. It grabbed the line in its beak and walked backward, pulling up the line. The clever crow held the line down with its feet while it walked forward to grab the line farther down. When the fish finally reached the surface, the crow grabbed it and ate it.

What a complicated procedure for a bird to plan and carry out!

Curiosity in animals helps them to learn about their environment. Species with less curiosity tend to be less intelligent. Macaws, cockatoos, and parrots all have active curiosities and are almost as intelligent as crows.

All vertebrates can learn. Some of the lower vertebrates understand the meaning of numbers; some have curiosity, imagination, creativity; and some have the ability to solve difficult problems. Mammals are the highest order of the vertebrates. They possess all of these elements of intelligence, but to a much greater extent.

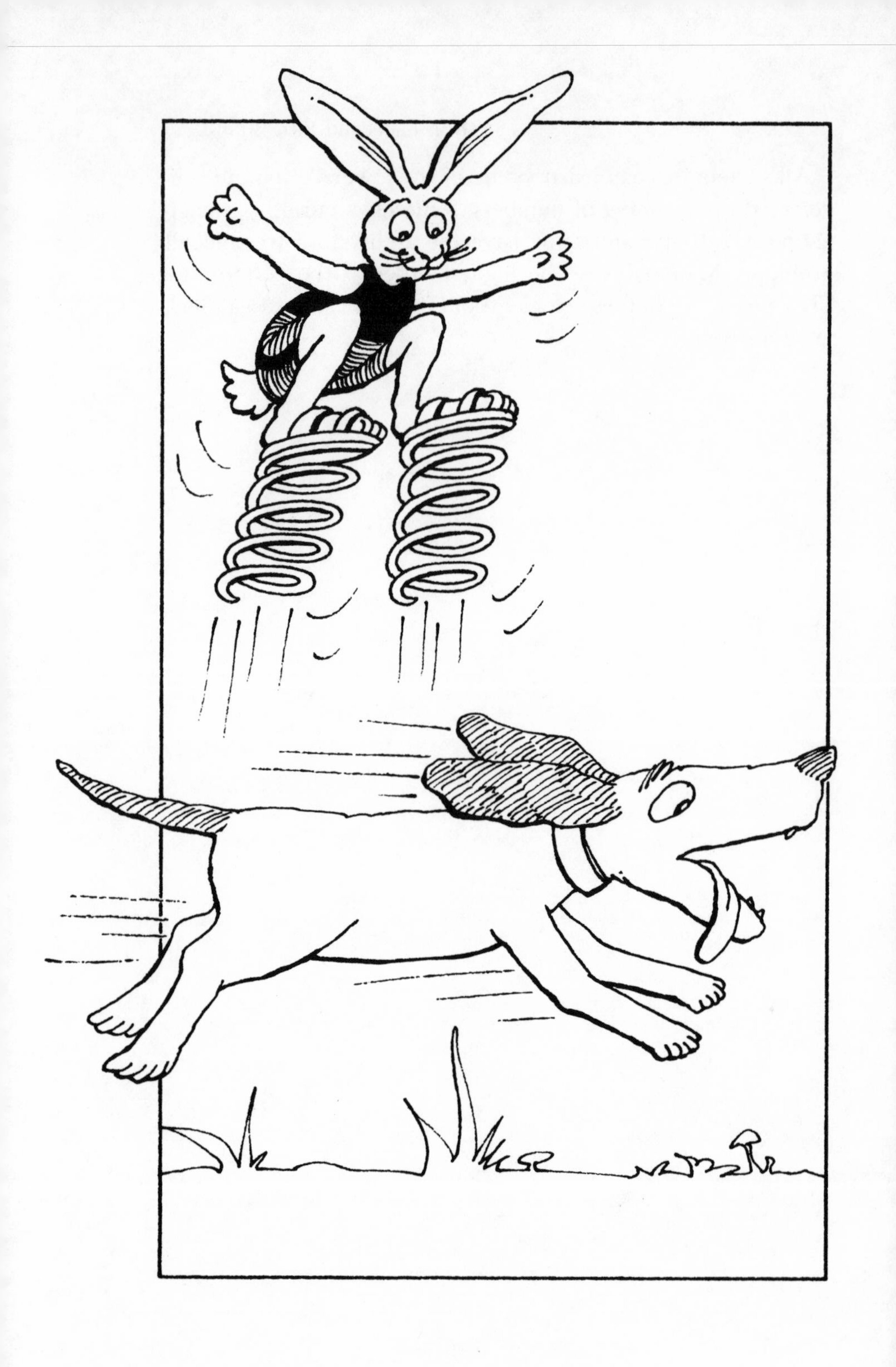

The Not-So-Dumb Wild Animals

Jackrabbits, like most mammals, are expert at defending themselves from natural enemies. Observers have seen them use more than one crafty trick to defeat a pursuing hound.

Often a jackrabbit will act as if it doesn't know a hound is trailing it, except that it occasionally gives a high bound and looks back to see what is going on. As the hound draws near, however, the rabbit picks up speed. Then when the dog is almost on top of the rabbit, the rabbit suddenly leaps straight up into the air. The dog does not expect this and is unable to stop suddenly. It rushes past. Whereupon the rabbit lands, doubles back, and escapes into a hollow log or briar patch.

Once a pursued rabbit was seen running alongside a deep ditch, the hound close on its heels. At the last instant, the rabbit jumped sideways across the ditch. Turning to follow, the dog plunged head over heels into the ditch, while the clever jackrabbit escaped into the sagebrush.

Sometimes two or more jackrabbits team up and run a dog to exhaustion. One jackrabbit runs until it is tired, then the second takes its place while the first rests. Decoying a dog into a barbed-wire fence is one of the jackrabbit's most deadly tricks. The rabbit waits until the dog is just behind it, then dives between the wires. The dog crashes into the fence, and is often seriously injured on the barbs.

The better an animal understands its environment, the more successful it is in obtaining food, avoiding capture, or winning a mate. Most mammals carry in their brains a mental map of their surroundings. This mental map, or memory, enables animals to adapt to changing situations and to alter their routes when the need arises. A rabbit knows every hollow log, hole in the fence, or briar patch in its territory. A mouse knows each brush pile or unused burrow that it can dive into if danger approaches.

Even insectivores, such as the hedgehog or shrew—which are not rated very high intellectually—are known for their ability to memorize every stick and stone in their paths. They quickly learn their territories but keep to the same route each time, although another way may be shorter. They do this because they have a limited ability to remember. Shrews are nearly blind and knowing every safe spot is necessary for their survival, just as a blind person needs to memorize every obstacle in his or her path.

Bats use sonar to find their way around in strange surroundings, but researchers have discovered that once a bat becomes familiar with its environment, it relies on its memory to get around, instead of using its sonar. Scientists tested this by allowing some bats to fly freely around a laboratory until they became thoroughly familiar with it. Then the scientists placed obstacles in the laboratory. The bats crashed into the barriers. They eventually learned from the experience, however, and went back to their sonar. They learned slowly, but that they were able to learn at all is important.

Opossums are not usually considered to be very bright. However, opossums learn quite well from experience. A pet opossum was once burned when it tried to climb a hot-water pipe. Thereafter, it always carefully patted the pipe before climbing it.

Scientists believe that animals living in social groups have a higher degree of intelligence than animals that live in small groups or lead lone lives. Mammals living in large social groups cooperate to perform tasks, and they share their food with one another. They even act as baby-sitters to help care for their young.

Prairie dogs have one of the highest social organizations of the lower mammals. Moreover, they have a complicated system of communication and are extraordinarily alert creatures with active curiosities. They are surely intelligent creatures.

Beavers cooperate and share to an even greater degree. Like all rodents, they store food for the winter. But unlike the mouse—who stores a year's supply of seeds for itself—beavers store food for the entire colony.

Beavers are best known for their engineering skills and dam building. With uncanny understanding of engineering principles, two beavers working together can build a 30-foot dam in a week. With teamwork, cooperation, and the ability to solve complicated problems, a family of beavers once built a dam in Montana that was 2,310 feet across. They had to cut trees far upstream and float them down to the treeless dam site.

Rats are believed to be the most intelligent members of the rodent family. Rats can run mazes better than humans and quickly learn to press the proper lever to obtain food. They can be taught to do several separate actions in order to get food, such as pushing a cart, climbing a tower, scurrying up a ramp, and pressing a lever. Later they are able to put all these steps

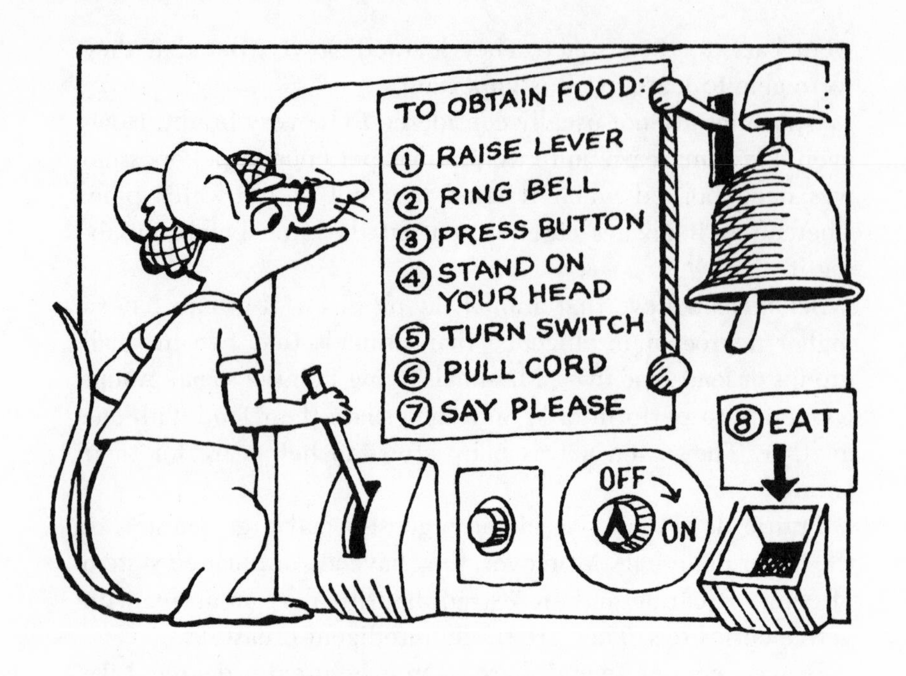

together, in sequence, for a single morsel of cheese. One very intelligent rat learned to go through a series of eight actions for a single reward.

Rats are clever at solving problems, too. In an experiment, dog biscuits were offered to some rats. The biscuits were too wide to fit between the bars of the cage. The crafty rats simply reached out with their paws, turned the biscuits sideways, and easily pulled them in.

Humans, the most intelligent animals on earth, have been outwitted by rats. In spite of people's attempts to trap and poison them, rats have increased in number. They either avoid traps entirely or kick them around until they go off, then eat the bait.

They will not eat poison because they have good memories and learn from their mistakes. They never again eat a food that once made them ill. Scientists think rats may be able to communicate this information to their young, because very few rats will touch poisoned bait.

Many mammals teach survival skills to their young. Bears have been known to shake their youngsters or box their ears if they do not pay attention to what is being taught. Mountain goats teach their young to be surefooted mountain climbers, but more importantly, they teach them how to escape the mountain lion.

Hoofed animals rely mostly on speed to escape predators, but they must also be able to use their wits because their enemies are large and skillful. Deer, for example, are very alert creatures. They pay close attention to everything that goes on around them and constantly watch for changes in the behavior of predators. From a predator's actions, a deer knows if it has eaten recently or if it is looking for food. And the deer knows exactly how close it can allow an enemy to approach and still be able to escape. Hoofed animals frequently use tactics similar to those of the jackrabbit to confuse pursuers.

Science writer Edward Edelson reported that once an exhausted deer, fleeing a hound, came across a herd of hogs in a clearing. The deer slipped into the center of the herd and walked along with them for a while, then escaped into the woods. It sprinted to safety while the pursuing hound lost its trail and began chasing the hogs.

Carnivores (meat eaters) are usually more intelligent than the herbivores (plant eaters) that they prey upon. Carnivores have slightly larger brains and more highly developed mental skills. To be successful at capturing prey, they must be able to scheme and to coordinate all their sensual information—smell, sound, and sight—with their memories of past experiences.

Most carnivores are too dangerous and unpredictable to be studied in the laboratory; therefore, what is known about them is from observation of wild animals. The big cats—lions, tigers, and pumas—are shrewd hunters. They learn their hunting tactics from their mothers.

Lions usually hunt alone, but one ethologist (a person who studies animals) reported seeing several lions hunting together. Two lions circled a herd of antelopes and drove them toward a place where other lions were hidden in tall grass. One of the hidden lions then dashed in and scattered the prey, making it easy for the others to capture one.

Cheetahs may be the most intelligent members of the cat family. They are the only wild cats that can be tamed. For centuries, rajahs in India have trained cheetahs to hunt. At least one pet cheetah was shrewder than a hound. It soon learned to anticipate a jackrabbit's sudden leap into the air and stood underneath as the rabbit came down and caught it in its open mouth.

Wolverines are widely known for their shrewdness. These thirty-pound carnivores sometimes drop moss from a tree limb to lure a deer into ambush. When the curious deer goes to investigate, the wolverine leaps on it. Although wolverines usually hunt alone, they sometimes team up to drive deer into narrow gorges where they can be easily captured.

It is almost impossible to trap a wolverine. Trappers claim that these animals are almost as good as humans at figuring out the workings of mechanical devices. Wolverines have put many trappers out of business by carrying off the traps and destroying any prey that had been caught.

Members of the dog family—wolves, foxes, and coyotes—are omnivores. Although they mostly eat meat, they will eat plants and berries if meat is scarce. As a rule, omnivores are slightly more intelligent than carnivores. Foxes have a reputation for slyness, but actually wolves are smarter, and coyotes are even more intelligent.

Mexican farmers claim that coyotes are the smartest animals on earth. Their ability to survive under pressure indicates that they are indeed cunning creatures. They avoid poisoned foods and have been known to uncover every trap in an area and to take the bait without getting caught. Coyotes sometimes work in teams to exhaust hounds that are chasing them. They even have jumped on railroad trains to escape their pursuers.

Coyotes live by their wits and are resourceful hunters. They are particularly fond of prairie-dog meat, but prairie dogs are difficult to catch because they are so shrewd and are always on guard. However, coyotes are perfectly capable of planning a scheme to catch one.

Ernest Thompson Seton reported seeing a pair of coyotes sneak up to the edge of a prairie-dog town. One hid in the brush while the other walked into the town, sending the prairie dogs scurrying for their holes. After the last one had disappeared, the second coyote rushed forward and hid behind a log near one of the mounds. The first coyote strolled nonchalantly on through the town. Shortly, the prairie dogs poked their heads up to see if all was clear. When they saw their enemy leaving, they came out, sat on their mounds, and scolded. Then the second coyote grabbed the nearest prairie dog and shared it with its mate.

Coyotes are remarkably playful. Even adults play together. Play among adult animals is considered a sign of exceptional intelligence. Captive coyotes can solve puzzles and work out complex situations. The more difficult the problem, the better they seem to like it. Coyotes were once thought to be the most intelligent of the meat eaters.

Recent tests show that raccoons may be the most intelligent of the lower mammals. Psychologists have found that raccoons can easily pass several tests that even the smartest dogs can't. In fact, raccoons have passed many tests designed to measure the intelligence of monkeys.

Raccoons can solve problems almost as well as monkeys. They are just as clever at turning knobs to open doors, pulling corks out of bottles, or unscrewing bottle caps. And, like monkeys, nothing short of a padlock can hold a raccoon in a cage. It takes one only minutes to open a latch or bolt.

Laboratory raccoons love puzzle boxes and will go back into them just for the fun of operating the gadgets. A scientist designed a puzzle box that required a raccoon to operate seven different devices to get out. The raccoon had to depress two different levers, pull down a loop of string, lift a latch, slide a bolt, undo a hook, and press down a thumb latch. The raccoon got out in eight seconds!

In another test, a raccoon was chained by its neck to a stake. A dish of food was placed just beyond its reach. When the raccoon discovered that it couldn't reach the food with its forefeet, it turned around and grabbed the food with its hind feet. Scientists call this type of problem solving "insightful learning." It happens suddenly and is not based on previous experience. Only the most intelligent animals have insight.

Raccoons are clever at catching fish, a favorite food. One raccoon was seen sitting in shallow water, allowing minnows to hide in its thick fur. Then it quietly reached down and caught the minnows with its hands.

Mammals are alert, curious, and adept at solving problems. It

may be that they are more intelligent than lower vertebrates because they receive more care and training from their parents. The longer the young are cared for, the better they seem to learn. Studies show that domestic animals learn more and easier than their wild relatives. This may be due in part to a better diet, but it may also be because they receive more training.

PRESS
BUTTON
TO OBTAIN
FOOD

5

Our Four-Legged Friends

Camels are generally considered to be rather stupid creatures. But Dr. Hal Markowitz, a research director, was fond of camels. He thought that the camel in the Portland Zoo might be bored just standing around all day with nothing to do. So he built a machine that would make the camel work to get its food. Then he taught the camel to push a button with its nose to make food drop through a slot. The camel seemed to enjoy doing this.

Next Dr. Markowitz wondered how many times the camel would be willing to push the switch before the food dropped. When would the camel decide the food wasn't worth the effort? To find out, Dr. Markowitz gradually increased the number of times the switch had to be pressed before the food dropped through the slot—from once to more than ten times. After a while, the camel stopped pressing the button with its nose. It simply laid its chin against the switch and vibrated it rapidly. The switch was pressed a dozen times in a matter of seconds with no effort. Now that was smart!

Camels are cleverer than had been suspected. Because of their disagreeable dispositions, camels seldom form close ties with humans. However, Dr. Markowitz had noticed that mother camels show as much love and affection for their young as human mothers do. So he used love and understanding to bring out the best in the camel at the zoo.

Studies show that most animals respond to love just as humans do. Pets that receive lots of love show more kinds of behavior that are considered signs of intelligence than those that do not receive attention. But along with love, animals need mental stimulation. Like human children, animals become smarter if they are given the opportunity to learn through experiences or are introduced to new situations, and if they are allowed to satisfy their curiosity by investigating things.

Most animals have a desire to learn and, given the opportunity, will do so. Animals in the wild that cannot learn quickly do not survive. Domesticated animals that are raised in close quarters and are not given mental stimulation or are not allowed to investigate do not develop high mental abilities.

There has been a lot of argument about which domesticated animal is the smartest. One of the problems is that tests used to measure the intelligence of animals (or humans, for that matter) are not always true indications of the intelligence of the one being tested. For example, psychologists usually estimate the intelligence of an animal from the size of its brain in relation to its body size and from the animal's ability to run a maze to obtain food.

Based on these tests, the horse scores rather low. It has a small brain compared to its body size, and it does very poorly on mazes. But a maze is not a good test for a horse. Animals that have to hunt for food do well on mazes. A horse is a grazer who finds its food under its feet. It does not know how to look for food at the end of tunnels.

Many people believe that horses are more intelligent than such tests indicate. People who train horses for circuses or for riding or to do farm or ranch work say that some horses are very intelligent. They learn rapidly and remember what they learn. Others, they admit, learn slowly and don't remember well.

Almost all horses are alert and have keen curiosities, which definitely shows intelligence. And they love to play. Mares play with their colts to teach them lessons they must learn to be successful adults. When horses have little opportunity to play, they invent their own games. A horse prefers to play with another horse, but will play with a trainer or another animal if no other horse is available.

Show horses learn quite complicated tricks. Some even learn things that were not taught to them. One clever horse could give the answers to arithmetic problems by pawing the ground with its right front foot. If someone asked it the sum of seven and eight, it pawed fifteen times. Everyone, including the horse's master, thought the horse was actually solving the problems by itself. However, tests proved that although the horse could not actually add, it was really quite a clever horse. It had

learned to read its master's body language. That is, it could tell by very small changes in the master's expression or movements when it had the correct answer and stopped pawing at that point.

Many ordinary horses are just about as clever. Once a horse was seen using an empty feed sack as a fly swatter. Lots of horses fake lameness to get out of working. And many can untie knots and figure out how to lift the hatch on a stable door or unlock the most difficult gate latches.

A trainer thought that perhaps the stallion that had learned to slip the bolt on its stall door and couldn't be kept in was bored. So he tied a dozen knots in a long piece of rope and gave it to the horse. Using only its teeth, the stallion untied every knot in a few minutes. Then it slipped the bolt on its door, walked out, and handed the rope to its trainer.

This kind of behavior indicates a much higher degree of intelligence than tests show. So scientists began looking for better ways to measure the intelligence of horses. They discovered that some can actually count to seven. A horse in a zoo in Germany could tell the difference between twenty different pairs of designs. When it was retested three months later, it still remembered what it had learned. A zebra can tell the difference between only ten pairs of designs. These tests are much better indications of a horse's intelligence than a maze. They show that horses have excellent learning ability.

Domestic cats also score poorly in running mazes. Cats are too independent to cooperate in tests. They seldom will work for food and do not perform well on command.

However, anyone who has ever lived with a cat knows that cats are smart. And most psychologists agree that cats are fairly well up on the scale of animal intelligence. They easily get out of puzzle boxes. They are able to figure out even quite complicated hook and hasp latches, but are slower than raccoons. Of course, some cats are smarter than others. The Siamese is probably the most intelligent of the domesticated cats. But all cats are curious and have a fairly adaptable and alert mind. They communicate with their owners quite successfully. Some say cats use as many as sixty-three different sounds to communicate their needs. They can tell you when they want out, when they want in, or when they are hungry. Many will bang a screen door to tell you they want in—one learned how to bang a door knocker—and some have learned to open window latches and screen doors to let themselves in.

One cat has been credited with saving the lives of its human family. It waked its master by repeatedly jumping on his bed when the house caught on fire during the night.

Other cats have been known to set traps for birds. One took scraps of bread and placed them near a bush. Then it hid under the bush and waited for a bird to come down to get the bread. As soon as the bird lit on the ground, the cat pounced on it.

Cats can also count. If you take one kitten from a litter of six out of the box while the mother is away, she will miss the kitten when she returns and will look for it.

Experiments show that the more a kitten is played with in its first few weeks of its life, the more intelligent it will be when it is grown. Other tests show that cats learn quicker after they have watched another cat do something. However, a mother cat teaches her young to catch mice by allowing them to help her. This is a much better way to learn. A kitten or puppy taken from its mother before it is seven weeks old will not be as intelligent as one left longer.

Psychologists believe that cats are about as intelligent as dogs, even though they do not do as well on tests. Cats don't especially care to please.

Dogs, on the other hand, are very anxious to please. They are easily motivated—a very important ingredient for intellectual development. They will work for hours for nothing more than a pat on the head or a word of praise. They usually do quite well on laboratory tests.

Most dogs are alert and pay close attention to everything

around them, even keeping an ear cocked when sleeping. They are much better at reading body language than humans. They can detect the slightest change in the behavior of other animals or humans. That is how they know what you are going to do before you do it or when you dislike or are afraid of someone.

Almost any dog can be taught a few tricks for a reward—one learned 150. Many learn to do useful tasks for humans. Guide dogs and police dogs learn many difficult lessons and can remember them for life. Sheepdogs are especially intelligent. They can round up strays, bring in an entire flock of sheep, and separate marked sheep from a flock with just a few words of instruction.

Dogs are clever at communicating their needs. They nuzzle, whine, run to the door and scratch, look imploringly—all clearly making you understand that they want to go out. Some bring their supper dishes when they are hungry, or a ball when they want to play.

Dogs also have a high degree of receptive language (they know the meaning of spoken words, even though they can't say them). Most dogs understand at least twenty-five commands. Well-trained dogs learn one hundred or more. One is said to have understood five hundred commands. Intelligent dogs that live many years in close association with people may understand almost anything said to them.

A few dogs have been taught to spell. One used letters it selected from a card rack to spell words that were dictated to it. Elizabeth Borgese taught a dog named Arli to spell twenty words within six months. Arli then learned to spell several closely related words. He typed the words on a specially built typewriter that had very large keys. Arli punched the keys with his nose.

A physical therapist who worked with spastic children learned about the dog and its special typewriter. Many of her patients had such poor coordination that they couldn't write, because they couldn't hold a pencil or operate a regular type-

writer. Some couldn't even speak. The therapist thought that her children could do what Arli could do. So she obtained two specially built typewriters for her children. The children soon learned to press the keys with whatever part of their bodies they could best control—feet, knees, elbows, or even hands. Their lives became much happier.

In the laboratory, dogs quickly learn to tell the difference between shapes. Scientists at the Pavlov Institute taught a dog the difference between a circle and an ellipse. Each time the dog chose the circle, it received a reward. When it chose the ellipse, it got nothing. Then the scientists gradually made the ellipse more and more like a circle. Still the dog was able to pick the circle every time—even when the scientists themselves could no longer see the difference. A dog's ability to see differences is greater than that of humans. Another dog learned to pick the correct design from nine different pairs of shapes. It took the dog only one week to learn to do this. The same dog could count to six.

The older a dog gets, the wiser it becomes. One animal psychologist thinks that dogs accumulate a file of knowledge in their brains that they can draw on to solve new problems as they are met. This seems to be true of humans, too.

Dogs and horses are clever, and cats are probably just as bright, but there are some who claim that pigs are more intelligent than any of them. A pig raised as a pet and given much love and attention will follow you around like a dog. Pigs naturally have insatiable curiosities and learn very quickly. They can learn to do anything that a dog can, and in less time. They have been taught to dance, tumble, fetch, pull a cart, bring in the cows, and even to sniff out land mines in combat zones. And they will do all this for a simple reward of affection and food.

Unlike cats or dogs, pigs do independent thinking. Scientists say that pigs solve problems by thinking them through. Pigs easily learn to open locks and gates and to climb fences. They are also extraordinarily communicative, using grunts and squeals to make their wants or needs known.

Scientific tests show, however, that elephants are the most intelligent of the domestic animals. People who work with these animals have always claimed that elephants are very intelligent creatures. The elephant's jumbo-size brain is four times larger than a human brain. Generally the larger the brain, the smarter the animal, but an elephant weighs fifty times as much as a human, and in comparison to its body weight, the elephant's brain is much smaller than that of a man. And, of course, the elephant is much less intelligent.

Nonetheless, elephants are said to be next to primates and porpoises in intelligence. They are also among the most adaptable animals. Being able to adjust to changing situations is important to successful living. It requires a special kind of intelligence to be adaptable. Elephants are the only animals that can be successfully domesticated after they have reached adulthood. But love, understanding, and kindness are required to train elephants successfully.

Elephants have great affection for one another and especially for their young. Once a young male elephant got trapped in a deep mud hole in Kenya. It couldn't get out because the banks were too steep. While two game wardens watched, three bull elephants rescued the young male by trampling down the sides

of the hole to form a ramp. Then they pulled the young elephant to safety. Don't you think that was clever?

Mother elephants teach their young everything they know. This is a big advantage. Scientists have discovered that the more any youngster—animal or human—is taught, the more it can learn. Elephant calves have a long childhood in which to learn. They stay with their mothers for about sixteen years. Mother elephants show a great deal of tender affection for their young, but will discipline the youngsters by spanking them with their trunks if they disobey.

Most elephants understand human language very well and respond to thirty or forty commands such as "lift your foot," "go forward," "push with your foot," and "kneel." One smart elephant learned one hundred different commands. But an elephant's ability to work without instruction is even more remarkable.

Some elephants seem to be able to look over a problem, then use their heads to solve it. Lumbermen in Africa claim that elephants figure things out the same way humans do.

Elephants that work in the lumber camps of southeast Asia and Africa do very complicated tasks with little supervision. They stack logs neatly in piles and seem to understand where to place each log so that the whole pile doesn't come tumbling down. They carry logs to log slides and maneuver them carefully into position with their trunks, then give the logs a push with their forefeet and watch as the logs splash into the water below. To do all this, they need only one simple command.

A trainer can tell an elephant that he wants an area cleared. The elephant will set to work uprooting trees, pushing them with its head until they lean, then shoving them to the ground with a forefoot. If roots prevent a tree from falling, the elephant walks around the tree and pulls out the roots without being told to.

One investigator claims that only chimpanzees and orangutans can learn tricks better than elephants. Circus elephants have learned to balance on a rolling ball, perform on a seesaw, ride a bicycle, and even play cricket. An elephant can remove a cork from a bottle and fold a cloth like a napkin with its trunk. Moreover, elephants seem to enjoy doing their tricks. Once a female was seen practicing when she thought no one was watching. Apparently, doing tricks is like playing to an elephant, and elephants love to play. One favorite game of young elephants in India is sliding down grassy slopes on their backsides.

Scientists say that some of the ways in which elephants solve problems come very close to reasoning. An elephant in the Ringling Brothers circus performed a stunt that required her to sit on a tub. One day the tub tipped and caused the elephant to fall in front of the audience. After that, the elephant refused to sit on the tub. Her trainer kept after her until she finally sat on the tub again. At least everyone thought she did—until it was discovered that the elephant wasn't actually sitting on the tub. She was just lowering herself down to within an inch of the tub and holding a sitting position through the whole performance!

A scientific test proved the old saying, "Elephants never forget." Professor Les Squier trained elephants in the Portland Zoo to press lighted panels with their trunks to get food. But the project was soon stopped because of a lack of money. Eight years later, zoo employees found the old test equipment and took it to the elephant house. They were astonished when a Vietnamese elephant that had participated in the experiment began pressing the panels as if she had been practicing every day!

Professor Bernard Rensch decided to find out how much an elephant can learn. He placed two boxes in front of an elephant. The lid of one box was marked with a black cross, the lid of the other with a black circle. The elephant received a piece of bread if it chose the lid marked with a cross; it got nothing if it chose the one marked with a circle. It took the elephant several days to learn this, but after that, it chose only the cross. Then Dr. Rensch taught the elephant to pick the correct pattern from other pairs. Once it got the idea, the elephant learned each new pair more and more quickly. The elephant surprised everyone by learning the difference between twenty pairs of patterns before the tests were stopped. A year later, the elephant was retested on thirteen pairs of the patterns. It remembered twelve of them correctly. It forgot only the most difficult one.

Dr. Rensch also discovered that the elephant could tell the difference between pairs of short melodies as well as it could with patterns. Elephants have absolute pitch—something that only the most gifted human musicians have. If an elephant is taught to look for food when it hears a B note, it will not look for food when it hears B-flat or B-sharp, only when it hears a pure B note. Elephants appreciate music and beat out rhythms with their feet. Circus elephants love to dance, and even wild elephants dance in the jungle.

All in all, elephants appear to be truly intelligent creatures. But there are many levels of intelligence. A person who works with his hands has a different kind of intelligence than one who works with the mind. Similarly, elephants have a different kind of intelligence than dogs or horses. Domestic animals in general learn more and learn faster than most wild animals, but they learn much less and much slower than primates or porpoises.

Many things contribute to the intelligence of an animal: physical health and good environment—love, attention, stimulation, and close contact with others—are important. Domestic animals that are well taken care of are usually healthier than wild animals. They usually have a more stimulating environment with lots of love and attention. A good environment cannot give an animal (or a human) an ability it does not possess, but it does give the animal a better chance to become smarter. Every animal is born with potentials that are never used. Love and stimulation bring out many of these latent talents.

Primates, the highest form of land mammals, receive more love and care during infancy and childhood than all other mammals (except humans). They are much more intelligent than other nonhuman mammals.

Primates—Mental Giants of the Animal World

A small monkey named Hellion took some food from a refrigerator and fed her master his lunch. Next, on command from her master, she turned out the kitchen light and went into the living room where she began dusting the furniture.

Hellion is a female capuchin monkey. She is part of an experiment at the Albert Einstein College of Medicine. There capuchins are being trained to serve as aides for people who are confined to wheelchairs and who cannot use their arms. The scientists hope that the monkeys will be as helpful for quadriplegics as guide dogs are for the blind.

Capuchins were chosen for this project because they are the smartest of the monkeys, and no one doubts the intelligence of a monkey. They learn rapidly and have good memories. Their brains are twice as large (in comparison to their body size) as the brains of dogs or raccoons. And their brains are more highly developed. Other primates are more intelligent, but their large size makes them inappropriate as aides. They become too unpredictable and unruly when they reach maturity. Monkeys are much easier to control, even though they are extremely curious and playful. Monkeys love to tease, and any object that is new to them must be investigated—and taken apart if possible.

A professor once gave some rhesus monkeys a mechanical puzzle just to see what they would do with it. The monkeys were fascinated with it and worked it again and again, even though they received no reward for solving it. The challenge was reward enough. Unfortunately, the more intelligent a monkey is, the more curious it is and the more destructive it can be.

Psychologists have devised many kinds of tests to measure the intelligence of primates. Monkeys love tests and work hard at solving them. When they master a problem, they tend to get cocky and boisterous. But when they can't solve the problem, they quickly become frustrated, and if the equipment isn't bolted down, they might attempt to throw it out of a window!

Researchers wondered how well young monkeys could do, compared to young children. They tested a group of preschool children. Then they gave the same test to a group of young monkeys. The children as a whole did better on the test than the monkeys, but the smartest monkeys did better than the slowest children. When the monkeys were retested a year later, they were able to do the tests quickly, indicating that they also have good memories. Some monkeys have done better than humans on certain memory tests.

Adult monkeys score better than human children on some kinds of difficult problem-solving tests. Monkeys appraise a situation, looking it over carefully, and proceed to solve the problem without trial and error. Scientists call this "insight behavior"—a sign of very high intelligence.

Scientist W. E. Galt showed some cards marked with both black and white dots to several monkeys. When the monkeys correctly matched two cards that were exactly alike, they received a grape or raisin. Most of the monkeys appeared to be guessing at their answers. But the capuchin monkeys looked at each card carefully before making a choice. They scored much better on the test than the other monkeys. This seems to indicate that the capuchins were truly thinking about the problem before making a decision.

Monkeys master puzzle boxes quickly. Scientists use puzzle boxes to test an animal's ability to reason. Usually the animal is placed inside a wire box with a door. A dish of monkey's favorite food is placed outside in plain sight. To get the food, the monkey must figure out how to open the door. It may need to press a lever, pull a string, jerk a chain, step on a pedal, tear away paper, or something similar. Sometimes several combinations of actions are required.

Scientists learn even more about monkeys' intelligence by watching them solve their own problems. Gibbons at the Portland Zoo had been taught to pull a lever whenever a certain light came on. This caused a light beside another lever to flash on. When that lever was pulled, food dropped from a slot in the wall. Harvey, the brightest monkey, became the chief lever puller. The only problem was that his cage mates simply sat beside the food slot and waited for the slices of apple to drop when Harvey pulled the second lever. However, Harvey soon caught on. After that, he pulled the second lever only when the other monkeys were far away from the food slot.

In another case, diana monkeys were taught to pull two chains when a light came on. The second chain caused a token to drop. The token had to be placed in a vending machine. In this case, the monkeys cooperated in pulling the chains. A young male pulled the first chain, and his mother pulled the second and got the token. However, she didn't know how to operate the vending machine, so she dropped the token onto the floor and the young male put it into the slot. Pieces of apple emerged, but before he could get them, his mother dashed over and grabbed them. The next time the light came on, the little monkey pulled the first chain, his mother pulled the second, got the token, and dropped it on the floor. The little monkey picked it up, but he didn't go near the vending machine. He nonchalantly strolled around the cage as if he didn't know what he was supposed to do. Finally, when his mother's back was turned, he dashed to the vending machine and deposited the token!

Baboons, one of the few primates that eat meat, team up to catch prey. They take turns chasing the prey—usually a young gazelle or rabbit—which is a swifter runner than the baboons. When the first baboon gets tired, a second one takes its place. Then when the second gets tired, a third takes its place. Always there is a fresh baboon chasing the prey, which eventually becomes so exhausted that it is easily caught.

The macaque monkeys on a tiny Japanese island had another kind of problem. Scientists fed them by dumping potatoes and grain onto a sandy beach. Sand on the potatoes hurt the monkeys' teeth. One female solved the problem by taking her potato to the shore and scrubbing it clean in the water. Several juvenile monkeys saw her and began imitating her. Soon most of the young monkeys on the island washed the sand off their potatoes before eating them.

Another smart monkey on the island separated the grain from the sand by throwing a handful of grain into the water of a stream. The sand sank to the bottom, while the grain floated.

The monkey ran downstream and caught the clean grain as it floated by. Other monkeys imitated this method also.

These monkeys used truly creative thinking to solve their problems. Most monkeys are creative in some way. This can be seen in the games they play and the mischief they get into. However, one capuchin monkey that was exceptionally vocal showed creativity in a more advanced way. Without any prompting or training, it began sketching pictures on the concrete floor of the laboratory, using a nail to draw sets of lines in orderly patterns. It seemed to know what it wanted to draw and became distressed if disturbed. Scientists consider this monkey a subhuman genius.

Monkey language can be quite expressive. A psychologist once trained a monkey named Trader to trade marbles for bits of food. After the monkey learned to do this, the psychologist began taking the marbles without giving the monkey anything in return. At first, the monkey acted puzzled. The next time this happened it acted irritated. The third time, Trader howled in rage and screamed in monkey language that it had been cheated.

Vocal communication was once believed to be something that only humans could do and was considered to be the highest sign of intelligence. Scientists now know that all primates use oral communication along with signs and touch.

The communication system of the great apes is more complicated than that of monkeys, but even monkeys have a well-developed system. They bark or shriek alarms to warn others of their group when danger approaches. The cry tells not only that danger is present but also whether the danger is from a large mammalian predator, an eagle, or a snake. It also tells where the danger is coming from.

Of all the primates, the great apes—orangutans, chimps, and gorillas—are the most intelligent. The great apes have relatively large brains that are amazingly like our own. They have long periods of very close mother-infant contact. Throughout their long childhood (eight or ten years), they stay close to their mothers and learn everything they need to know by watching her. Young primates have inquisitive minds and are interested in everything that goes on around them. Therefore, they learn quickly. The great apes have a relatively long adult life span—forty to fifty years—in which to learn and have much to teach their young.

There is disagreement among scientists about which of the three great apes is the smartest, but it is generally agreed that the chimpanzees and gorillas are brighter than orangutans. However, recent studies show that orangutans are not far behind.

Most orangutans break off tree branches to use as umbrellas in heavy downpours. And one or two have been known to break

off the end of a stick and use it as a back scratcher. But otherwise, wild orangutans are not known to use tools. However, captive orangutans are incredibly clever at learning to use human tools. They can even open a child-proof medicine bottle. Dr. Biruté Galdikas, world authority on orangutans, reported seeing a young formerly captive orangutan make a digging tool by breaking a stick to form a sharp point.

Dr. Galdikas studied orangutans in the jungles of Borneo for ten years. She also helped return formerly captive orangutans to the jungle. At first, the former captives lived in Dr. Galdikas's home while she rehabilitated them by teaching them the things they needed to know in order to live in the jungle. But the orangutans were so destructive, Dr. Galdikas and her husband were forced to build an ape-proof house. They decided to move into the new house before the glass for the windows had arrived. The window openings were too high for the orangutans to reach. The orangutans were unhappy about being shut out and set up a howl. All but one. That one took just two minutes to find a way in. He dragged a stick to one of the windows, leaned it against the wall, and climbed in!

Dr. Galdikas wished that she could talk to these extremely intelligent animals and find out what was important to them. She knew that scientists had had good luck teaching other apes to use sign language. Dr. Gary Shapiro, a scientist from the University of Oklahoma, had taught captive orangutans a symbolic language using plastic symbols. And he had taught American Sign Language (the sign language used by deaf people) to captive chimpanzees. But no one had ever taught a sign language to a primate in its native habitat before. Dr. Galdikas was sure that her rehabilitated orangutans could learn sign language. So she invited Dr. Shapiro to come to Borneo and try to teach the American Sign Language to them.

Dr. Shapiro began his work with a female adult named Rinnie. This former captive had already been rehabilitated and had been living in the jungle for quite some time. However, she still came every day to eat at a feeding station. It was there that Dr. Shapiro went to give her lessons. Although Rinnie could come and go as she pleased, she seemed to enjoy the lessons and stayed for an hour or more each day. Within a few weeks, she could use signs and put them together to form sentences. Mostly her sentences had something to do with food—asking for something to eat: "Give more food," or "Gary give food." By the end of the first year, she had learned to use twenty different signs.

Dr. Shapiro had even better luck with a second orangutan. Princess was a very young female captive that had only recently been brought to the camp to be rehabilitated. Dr. Shapiro adopted Princess as a daughter and carried her everywhere. With all this loving attention, the little orangutan learned to use thirty signs within a year. She used them correctly in many more situations than did Rinnie.

Both Princess and Rinnie learned sign language just as quickly as captive chimpanzees and gorillas of the same age. Some scientists think that more study of these "people of the forest," as the name *orangutan* means in Malay, will prove that they are as intelligent as other great apes.

FISHING FOR BUGS

7

Primate Geniuses

A large male chimpanzee stopped to drink from a pool of water in the crotch of a tree. He sipped all that he could reach with his lips. Then he gathered a handful of leaves and chewed them until they became spongy. He dipped the "sponge" into the rest of the water and sucked out the moisture until the water was all gone.

The first time Jane Goodall, a scientist who studied chimpanzees in the jungles of Africa for many years, saw a chimpanzee do this, she was astonished! Here was a wild animal actually taking a natural object and changing it into something else, then using it as a tool. Only humans were supposed to be able to do that!

Chimpanzees are incredibly intelligent and are skillful tool users. Besides making sponges, with which they also collect honey and clean dirt from their bodies, chimpanzees make fishing rods. They strip leaves from a twig, vine or sprig of grass and poke the stem into the holes of ant or termite nests. Then they pull it out covered with the insects, which the chimpanzees consider very tasty. Chimpanzees also use sticks or twigs to gather food or to pick their teeth. And once a chimpanzee was seen extracting a tooth with a twig.

Many scientists think that chimpanzees are the smartest animals that have ever lived—next to man, that is.

Most of the higher mammals have some capacity for reasoning and the ability to solve problems. As we saw in chapter 1, Dr. Koehler discovered that chimpanzees not only reason, they also use tools to solve problems. This suggests a much higher degree of intelligence than it was supposed any animal had.

In one experiment, Dr. Koehler placed food outside a chimpanzee's cage and beyond its reach. The chimp picked up a stick and dragged the food close enough to grab. Another time, a chimp broke off a branch to make a stick for pulling in food. In still another experiment, Dr. Koehler placed two short, hollow bamboo rods in the chimp's cage. Neither stick was long enough to reach the food. But the smart chimp fastened the two rods together by pushing the narrower rod into the end of the other and used it to rake in the food.

If boxes are placed in their cage, most bright chimps will stack them to reach a banana placed above their heads. One stacked four boxes to get the banana. Dr. Koehler observed that chimpanzees carefully study a problem for a while, then arrive at a solution to the problem quite suddenly.

Chimpanzees learn very quickly. Those raised in captivity understand human language quite well and can be trained to do almost anything. They can saw wood, hammer nails, use a screwdriver or a fork and spoon, unlock a padlock with a key, and untie knots. A chimp raised on a farm in Mississippi could start and drive a tractor, plow fields, and feed cattle. And, of course, chimps are great performers in circuses and on televi-

sion. Sometimes they show real creativity in their performances.

All chimpanzees are creative in the most general sense of the word. That is, they arrive at new solutions to new or old problems and can make things happen the way they want them to. This has been well demonstrated by many experiments. In addition, chimps are creative in an artistic sense. Wild chimps perform rain dances whenever it rains. They break off tree limbs and stomp around on two legs, brandishing the boughs.

Some captive chimps have more artistic talent than many humans. Two chimpanzees became famous when their paintings were exhibited in a London art gallery. Congo, a male at the London Zoo, would rather paint than eat. He was never given art lessons but was provided with materials and shown how to hold a brush. Although Congo never drew recognizable objects, his paintings were very pleasing, well-composed, and filled all of the space on the paper. Congo seemed to know exactly what he wanted to do and became distressed if disturbed or interrupted before he had finished.

Chimpanzees have excellent memories. A scientist tested a chimp's memory by allowing it to watch him bury a pear. Sixteen hours later, he freed the chimpanzee. It went directly to the place where the pear was buried and retrieved the fruit.

Like monkeys, chimps love tests. They have been given many standardized tests designed for human children. In one of these tests, they are required to place square, round, and triangular blocks in holes of the same shapes. Chimpanzees learn to do this faster than most children.

Most IQ tests for humans have several questions for determining a person's ability to tell the differences or similarities between objects. This is difficult to do and is therefore a good measure of high-level intelligence. Chimps are experts at this kind of test.

One smart chimp could tell the difference between fourteen different geometric figures such as squares, circles, and hexagons. It could also tell the differences between ten solids—spheres, cylinders, cubes and pyramids.

A Russian psychologist placed wooden triangles, squares, and circles in a bag. Then she taught a chimpanzee to feel in the bag and pull out a piece that was shaped like one that she held up. This clever chimp was able to match something it saw to something it felt.

Sarah, a fourteen-year-old chimp at the Primate Center of the University of Pennsylvania, can tell the differences in amounts of liquid. More importantly, she can determine if the amounts are the same, even when the shape changes. A scientist poured the same amount of tinted water into two identical jars. Then he asked the chimp if the amounts were the same or different. The chimp answered "same" by placing a plastic symbol representing the word *same* on the tray. Then the water was poured from one of the jars into a larger jar. This changed the shape of the water. But Sarah had seen the scientist pour the water into the second jar and knew that the second jar still held the same amount as the first.

Most small children would have said that the two jars were different, because one column of water was taller than the other. Older children know the amount remains equal, even though the shape changes. Sarah did just as well with solids. When shown two clay columns of equal size and shape, she knew they were still equal when one was smashed flat. This kind of ability requires a high level of intellectual maturity.

Recent tests show that Sarah is good at other kinds of math also. If shown two cupfuls of water and asked to match the amounts, Sarah can select two apples or two disks as being equal in number. But more remarkable, the chimpanzee knows that ¼ of an apple or ¼ of a wooden disk is equal in proportion to ¼ cup of water; ½ of an apple is equal to ½ cup of water; and ¾ of a wooden disk is equal to ¾ cup of water. Very few six-year-old children can do this well with fractions.

Sarah's trainer, Dr. David Premack, showed her a series of videotapes. The tapes depicted human actors trying to solve simple problems. For example, on one of the tapes a man was trying to get a banana that was hanging out of his reach. On another, he was trying to wash a cage with a hose that was not connected to a faucet.

After watching each tape, Sarah was shown four different pictures. Only one gave the correct solution to the problem. Sarah chose the right picture every time—an actor stacking boxes under the banana for the first, and the actor fastening the hose to the faucet for the second. Sarah did better than five-year-old children. She was also able to match two pictures, one of a whole apple and one of a cut apple, with the tool that caused the change.

Is Sarah naturally more intelligent than other apes? Or did her training have something to do with her intelligence? Sarah has had extensive training, including exercises in the use of language. Scientists believe that the ability to think and the ability to see the difference between things is at least partly a result of training. Some suggest that the intelligence of the great apes may be partly due to their long childhood. Generally, the more helpless an animal is at birth, and the more it has to learn to be able to take care of itself, the more intelligent it tends to be as an adult. Likewise, humans and animals who get more training and experience in meeting problems before they become adults are better thinkers.

Scientists thought that they should be able to teach chimpanzees to speak, because chimps are quite intelligent and understand many words spoken to them. Among humans, the number of words a person knows and can use correctly is considered one of the best measures of intelligence. Speech in human children develops as a result of close contact with older humans and constantly hearing language. Therefore, several psychologists decided to take baby chimps into their homes and raise them as if they were human children. They hoped to teach the chimps to talk by speaking to them regularly.

At first, the baby chimps made rapid progress. They learned to do most things faster than human children. And they seemed to understand just about everything that was said to them. But only one ever learned to speak, and she could say only four words—*mama, papa, cup,* and *up.* Chimps, it was learned, have difficulty forming words. They do not have the proper speech organs. As soon as human children learn to speak, they rapidly pull ahead of chimpanzees in mental development. Although they could not speak, the young chimpanzees could make their families understand most of their needs through gestures and pantomime.

Since wild chimpanzees also use a great many gestures and arm movements to communicate with one another, Beatrice and Allen Gardner decided to take advantage of this natural ability. They began to teach ASL (American Sign Language) to

Washoe, a chimpanzee at the University of Nevada. They spoke to Washoe every day, but only in sign language. This experiment was a success. Washoe soon learned to use 160 signs. She could form sentences and often invented words of her own in ASL. She called a watermelon a "drink fruit." A swan was a "water bird," and her word for refrigerator was "food-drink." Once she called a monkey that had threatened her "dirty monkey." Since Washoe had never been spoken to in English, she never learned the meaning of spoken words.

Washoe is now an adult and is teaching a younger chimpanzee at Central Washington University to use sign language. So far, she has taught the two-year-old fourteen sign words.

Several other chimpanzees have been taught sign language. Nim and Ally each learned 150 signs at the Institute for Primate Study at the University of Oklahoma. Their teacher, Dr. Roger Fouts, also taught sign language to Lucy, a home-raised chimp. Lucy had a vocabulary of more than one hundred words, and she understood many English words as well.

Like most chimpanzees, when Lucy matured, she became difficult to manage. Lucy's human parents had to make a choice. They could either keep Lucy locked in a cage for the rest of her life or set her free in the jungle. They decided to send her to Africa with another ex-captive.

Janis Carter, a graduate student and one of Lucy's teachers, volunteered to go with Lucy and help her and her companion learn to live in the jungle. Since Lucy had been born in captivity, she had a lot to learn. But she was a smart chimpanzee, and Janis was sure she could do it. However, it wasn't to be easy.

One of the first things Lucy had to learn was to find food in the jungle. Most of a chimpanzee's food grows on trees, so Janis put tasty blossoms on a platform high in a tall tree.

The other ex-captive climbed the tree to eat, but Lucy objected. The tree trunk was thick, and she was used to having her food brought to her.

She signed to Janis, "More food, you go," and she pointed to the top of the tree where her companion and several other former captives were enjoying a feast.

"No," said Janis.

Lucy took Janis by the hand and led her to the base of the tree. She placed Janis's hands on the trunk. Then she repeated, "More food, Janis go."

Janis refused, and Lucy finally climbed the tree with the help of a board propped against the trunk.

Eventually Lucy began to enjoy her life as a free chimp. She had to learn a whole new language. The other chimpanzees could not understand her signs, so she stopped trying to talk to them in sign language and learned to use the language of wild chimpanzees.

Sarah, Dr. Premack's smart chimpanzee, has a vocabulary of 130 words, but in a different kind of language. She understands a great many spoken words. Instead of American Sign Language, Dr. Premack taught Sarah a symbolic language. He used small plastic pieces of different shapes and colors—each representing a word. The symbols have metal strips on the back so that Sarah can form sentences by placing the symbols on a magnetic blackboard.

Sarah can read the sentences she makes and those that her teachers make. She also recognizes sentences that are similar in meaning and those that are different. Dr. Premack placed the symbols for two sentences on the blackboard: "Apple is red" and "Red color of apple." Sarah placed the symbol "same" beside them.

Then Dr. Premack placed two more sentences on the blackboard: "Apple is red" and "Cherry is red." Sarah placed "different" beside the two sentences.

Sarah did so well on the blackboad that Dr. Premack wondered if she could do as well on paper. He drew the symbols forming two sentences on several different sheets of paper. Then he drew the symbols representing "same" and "different" below the sentences. He gave Sarah a pencil and told her to mark the correct word for each set. Sarah got almost all of them correct!

Lana, a chimpanzee at the Yerkes Regional Primate Research Center, was taught a computerized language called "Yerkish" by Dr. Duane Rumbaugh. Like the language that Sarah learned, Yerkish is symbolic. But the symbols of Yerkish are written on a computer keyboard. Each symbol represents a word. When Lana punches a key, the symbol (or word) is flashed onto a screen. Lana knows 150 of these symbolic words. She has taught herself to read the sentences she writes. If she makes a mistake when writing a sentence, she erases it and starts over.

Once Lana saw a trainer eating an orange. She likes oranges, but she hadn't learned a symbol for the fruit yet. However, that didn't keep this smart chimp from asking for a bite!

She wrote, "Please, Tim, give apple that is orange."

Scientists have hoped that someday language-trained chimps would communicate with one another. Even chimpanzees that have not been taught a human language manage to give each other rather complicated information. Once a scientist showed a chimp where he had hidden some food. Then he put that one back in its cage and released several others. The other chimpanzees, who had not seen the hidden food, went directly to it. The first chimp had somehow managed to tell them where to find it. The scientists tried this several times with different chimps. Each time the others went directly to the food. But once, when the hidden food was something the first chimpanzee especially liked, it didn't tell the others where it was hidden. In fact, it seemed to try to keep them from finding the food!

In another experiment, a scientist placed a heavy box of food outside the cage of two chimpanzees, just beyond their reach. A rope was fastened to the box. One chimp pulled on the rope but couldn't move the box. It signaled the other chimpanzee to come and help. Together they pulled the box within reach and shared the goodies.

Lana's teachers decided to see if chimpanzees could communicate with one another in Yerkish. They placed two language-trained chimps, Sherman and Austin, in separate rooms. Each had a computer terminal. Dr. Rumbaugh let Sherman watch as he placed food in a box and padlocked it. Then he placed the box in Sherman's cage. Sherman didn't have the key, but he could see a key in a tray of tools in Austin's cage.

He went to his computer and typed, "Please, Austin give key."

Austin read his request and selected the key from the tray and gave it to Sherman. Sherman unlocked the box and shared its contents with Austin.

Now the Rumbaughs are using the same kind of keyboard to teach mentally retarded humans to communicate. In just a few weeks, one girl learned a vocabulary of 150 words. Even though her mental age is only that of a two-year-old, she learned Yerkish much faster than any chimpanzee. Her teachers are excited. Severely retarded people can learn much more than anyone ever thought they could. The girl's new ability to ask for things and to tell her teachers what she needs has completely changed her life. Now she is a happy person, eager to learn more. Before, all she did was rock and whimper all day.

It was once thought that gorillas could not learn. Gorillas don't do well on tests. They aren't interested in taking them or in mastering tricks. These shy animals don't enjoy showing off. They don't get the least upset when they can't solve a problem, so they don't try very hard.

Once a scientist tried to find out if a gorilla was smart enough to stack boxes to get a banana that was hung from the ceiling of its cage. The gorilla flunked the test. But like all gorillas, it liked its living quarters neat and clean. Although it wouldn't stack the boxes strewn around its cage to get the banana, it gathered them up and neatly stacked them in one corner to make the cage tidy.

Most tests for animal intelligence are mechanical in nature, and gorillas are not mechanically minded. The only tool that a

wild gorilla has ever been seen using is a crooked stick to pull food closer. Gorillas do break and bend tree branches into a rough platform for a nest, and they sometimes tie knots in young saplings to make the nest stronger. Dr. George Schaller once found a nest with twenty-four knots in it.

Most of what we know about gorilla intelligence is from observation rather than from testing. Drs. Schaller and Dian Fossey spent several years watching gorillas in the African jungle. They think that gorillas are just as intelligent as chimpanzees, and maybe smarter.

Other scientists agree. They point out that, of all the apes, a gorilla's body most closely resembles a human's, and gorillas act more like humans than do chimps—perhaps gorillas are closer to humans in intelligence also. Of course, it is true that gorillas are slow learners, but they are slow at everything. In the wild, they are unhurried and relaxed.

The first time Dr. Schaller saw a wild gorilla up close, he

wished there was some way he could tell it that he meant it no harm. Then he noticed that gorillas communicate with one another through an amazing number of gestures and vocal sounds. He began studying them and soon learned that when a gorilla shakes its head from side to side, it is saying, "I mean you no harm." After that, Dr. Schaller always shook his head when he met his gorilla friends. He also learned that a gorilla beating its chest is saying, "This is my territory. You are trespassing." And whenever a gorilla did this, he kept his distance.

Dian Fossey also wanted to talk to her gorilla friends. She studied their vocal sounds: the belching, growling, and hooting. She learned to say "Ho-ho-ho" to let them know that she was approaching. And she could warn them if danger was near or tell them if she found a new food source. But neither Dr. Schaller nor Dr. Fossey could carry on a conversation with the gorillas.

Many scientists thought that these extraordinarily humanlike animals ought to be able to learn to speak a human language. However, like chimpanzees, gorillas are not able to form words. So Dr. Francine "Penny" Patterson decided to try to teach American Sign Language to a gorilla. Dr. Patterson adopted Koko, a female baby gorilla that had been born in a zoo. She talked to Koko in English, but taught Koko to talk to her in sign language. By the time Koko was seven years old, she had learned 645 signs and used 375 of them regularly. Koko understands an even greater number of English words.

Koko can ask for anything she wants to eat or drink and can tell you what she wants to do. If she doesn't know the name for something, she invents one. She calls a mask an "eye hat," and a zebra is a "white tiger."

Koko is a fun-loving gorilla that likes to tease. Once her teacher was trying to show her off. She told Koko to touch different parts of her body as she named them. Koko wouldn't cooperate and kept touching the wrong places.

"Bad gorilla!" scolded her exasperated teacher.

"Funny gorilla!" signed Koko with a grin.

Another time, Koko was feeling contrary and wouldn't make the sign for "drink." Finally her teacher threatened to punish her if she didn't behave. Koko make a perfect "drink" sign, but in her ear instead of her mouth! Again there was a wide grin on Koko's face.

Humor is generally considered something that only humans possess. But Koko enjoys her little jokes. She also appreciates the practical jokes of her teachers, signing "That funny" when one of them clowns around. This suggests a higher level of intelligence than most people thought possible for gorillas.

Koko's teachers know when Koko is being deliberately disobedient. She doesn't have a grin on her face. Sometimes when Koko gets caught in mischief, she tries to lie her way out of it.

One day, Koko swiped a chopstick from a drawer and tried to poke a hole in the window screen with it. Penny saw her.

"Koko, what are you doing?" she asked.

Koko put the chopstick in her mouth and pretended to smoke it.

"I was smoking," she signed.

Sometimes when Koko breaks something she blames it on one of her teachers. Scientists think Koko's lying and fondness for pretending are indications of high intelligence. It shows that she knows what will happen if she is caught.

Occasionally Koko gets angry when she is not allowed to do something she wants to do or is pressed too hard on her lessons. Usually she just insults her teacher. She once called Penny, "Penny-toilet-dirty-devil!" But once she bit Penny. Penny scolded her, and Koko signed, "It's only a scratch."

It was, but Koko had to be taught not to bite, so she was sent to stand in a corner for a while.

Three days later, Penny talked to Koko about the bite.

"What did you do to Penny?" she asked.

"Bite," signed Koko. "Sorry bite."

"Why bite?" asked Penny.

"Because mad," answered Koko.

"Why mad?" asked Penny.

"Don't know," replied Koko.

It is very exciting to learn that an animal can remember something that happened several days before. When animals learn to communicate even better, what wonderful things might they be able to tell us?

Koko loves an argument. Once she signed, "That red." She held up a white towel.

"You know better than that, Koko," said her teacher. "What color is it?"

"Red, red, red," signed Koko. Then she held up a tiny bit of red lint that was caught on the towel.

Koko now has a playmate, a young male gorilla named Michael. Koko is helping to teach Michael sign language. Already he knows thirty-five signs, and the two gorillas sign to each other.

Koko is also learning a new way to communicate. She is being taught to use a special computerized keyboard similar to the one used by Lana, the chimpanzee. But when Koko presses the keys, her computer voices the words instead of flashing them onto a screen. This makes Koko a bilingual gorilla!

Gorillas may not do as well on tests as chimpanzees, but Koko is certainly not a stupid creature. When she was four years old, she was given an IQ test designed for human children. Koko scored ninety-five on the test. That is only slightly less than an average child does. The test was not an easy one for a gorilla to take. It had many of the same kinds of problems for Koko that such tests have for some children; what might be a correct answer for one child might not be for another or for a gorilla. For example, on one of the questions, Koko was shown pictures of an apple, a shoe, a flower, and an ice-cream sundae. Koko was told to point to two things that are good to eat. She pointed to the apple and the flower. According to the rules of the test, this was not a correct answer. But it was correct for a gorilla. Flowers are favorite foods of wild gorillas. On another question, Koko was asked where she would go for shelter in the rain. The pictures she was to choose from showed a house, a hat, a spoon, and a tree. Koko picked the tree. Being a gorilla, that is probably where she would go if given a chance. But, again, that was considered a wrong answer on the test.

Even though Koko was raised by a human, she knows that she is a gorilla. When she hears someone refer to her as a "juvenile" or an "adolescent," she quickly corrects that person.

"Koko fine gorilla," she signs.

Gorillas as well as chimpanzees recognize the image in a mirror as being their own reflection. All other animals act as if the image were another animal. The ability of these animals to recognize themselves shows that they have an awareness of self. Scientists think this may be one of the reasons they are able to learn language.

Some scientists question whether chimpanzees and gorillas are really using language. They say the animals are only imitating humans. Others say that even if chimpanzees and gorillas are only imitating, and even if they never learn to speak any better than they do right now, it is still a remarkable achievement. They have made far more progress learning our language than humans have in learning theirs.

Many scientists are investigating other areas of ape intelligence. They hope such studies will also help them learn how humans think. Some scientists suggest that we can outthink any other species because of our ability to write things down, which helps us to remember. Now that chimps and gorillas are learning to type and to read, will these skills increase their intelligence? Scientists want to know. They are working to find answers.

Other scientists are turning their attention to animals in the sea. Porpoises and whales have enormous brains. Animals with such big brains must have a rather high intelligence, they reason. We might learn more about intelligence by studying them.

Big Brains on the High Seas

A sea otter rolled onto its back to take a nap. It had carefully wrapped itself in a strand of kelp so that the ocean currents couldn't wash it out to sea or dash it against the rocky shores. Suddenly a net dropped over the sleeping otter. The otter struggled for a minute or two but soon stopped. It seemed to think about its predicament. Then it began to look for a way out of the net. First it tried to push the mesh apart. Next it tried to chew the net. But otters' teeth are designed for crushing shells of sea animals, not for cutting.

The otter's captors wanted to study this remarkably clever animal. They wanted to compare its intelligence with that of other mammals that live in the sea.

Marine mammals once lived on land, but long ago returned to the sea. Some have incredibly large brains. Scientists would like to find out how intelligent these animals are, but it is a very difficult task. Humans cannot live in their environment, and most of them cannot live in ours.

Unlike other marine mammals, sea otters have been living in the sea for only two hundred years. They still have legs and can easily walk and live on land, although few do. They returned to the sea to escape hunters. It is easier to escape sharks and killer whales in the sea than humans on land. Scientists hope that by studying sea otters they can begin to understand marine mammals that have been living in the oceans for millions of years.

Like most young marine mammals, sea otter pups live with their mothers for a long time and have a close relationship with them. They eat, sleep, and play on their mother's chest for a year, then are given survival training for another year. This increased attention and training has undoubtedly played a part in their mental development.

The netted otter used an intelligent approach to a serious problem. This shows that it is a smart animal.

Another indication of otter intelligence is their regular use of tools. Otters gather armfuls of shellfish from the ocean floor. Along with the clams and sea urchins, they bring back a large flat stone. When they reach the surface, they roll over on their back and eat a leisurely meal, using their belly as a table. Although they could easily crush the shells with their teeth, otters prefer breaking them open on the stone, which is placed on their chest. The shellfish are held in both paws and whacked against the stone.

After each clam is eaten, the otters roll over to wash away the crumbs, clasping any uneaten clams and the stone firmly under their arms. Then they return onto their back and finish their dinner.

As clever as otters are, they are not as smart as seals. Seals have been living in the ocean much longer. They learn so quickly and are so easily trained that they have long been favorites in circuses and zoos. When captured young and reared by humans, seals are even more affectionate than dogs. They learn

many complicated tricks including counting. Seals are especially fond of music and quickly learn to sing and play musical instruments.

Sea lions (eared seals) were the first sea animals ever taught to work for humans. The United States Navy trained them to locate test rockets in the Pacific Ocean. Each seal was taught to listen for a beep coming from the rocket. When it heard the beep, the seal pushed a rubber disk on the boat. Then the men fastened a grabbing device onto the seal's nose. The seal dived to the ocean floor and locked the grabber onto the rocket. The job done, the seal returned to the boat, and the rocket was lifted to the surface with a nylon line attached to the grabber.

Sea lions are so intelligent they quickly become bored if asked to do the same routine every day. The more intelligent an animal, the quicker it becomes bored. The sea lions at Sea World in Florida were so bored that they performed poorly and lost weight. To prevent boredom, the animals' environment was made more stimulating. Instead of fish for a reward, they received surprises. If a seal performs especially well, it gets a ride in a golf cart! The sea lions would rather earn a ride in the cart than work for all the fish they can eat.

The cetaceans—whales and dolphins (or porpoises as some people call them)—are the most intelligent of the marine mammals. They become bored very quickly. Everyone agrees they are intelligent animals, but opinions of how intelligent they are vary. Some people think cetaceans are no more intelligent than dogs. Others suggest that some cetaceans may be more intelligent than humans.

These scientists base their opinions on the size of the cetaceans' brains, which range from the size of an ape's brain, in a small dolphin, to one that is six times the size of a human's brain, in the sperm whale. Also, the part of a cetacean's brain that is larger than a human's is the cerebral cortex. This is the part that thinks, imagines, and plans. Generally, the larger the cerebral cortex, the more intelligent the animal. For example, human brains have larger cortexes than those of chimpanzees. Chimpanzees have larger cortexes than those of dogs. Cetacean brains also have more folds than the brains of humans. The number of folds in a brain is also associated with intelligence.

However, whether or not a cetacean is more intelligent than a human has not yet been proven. It is extremely difficult to measure a cetacean's intelligence, because it lives in an alien environment. Scientists usually measure the intelligence of an animal by its ability or skill in mastering problems with locks, mazes, and gadgets or by its proficiency in using tools. Whales can master a maze on the first trial, but since they have no hands, they cannot use tools or manipulate locks or gadgets. Still, we know that whales must be extraordinarily intelligent creatures, because they behave in extraordinarily intelligent ways.

Most scientists think that whales are about as intelligent as chimpanzees. They suggest that much of a whale's brain is used for handling its huge body. Others say that a whale's body grew large to protect its huge brain and that most of the whale's extreme size is blubber. Some suggest that cetaceans need large brains to process the sounds they hear. Certainly their world is full of sounds, and hearing is the most important sense they have. Like bats, cetaceans use sonar (they bounce sounds off objects) to find their way around the dark ocean waters and to find food. Perhaps whales need extra large brains to sort out all of those sounds.

Whales also communicate or "talk" with one another. Scientists have made tape recordings of their conversations. A whale's language consists of more than one thousand different sounds, including clicks, whistles, yelps, growls, and grunts. These sounds carry for a great many miles through the sea. Scientists are studying the tapes and watching how whales act when they make a particular sound. Others are using computers to try to decode the language of the whales. They want to find out what the whales are saying.

Humpbacks and right whales sing songs. They are the only mammals, other than humans, that sing true songs. When speeded up on a recorder, their songs sound like those of birds, but are much longer and louder. Some of the songs last for thirty minutes.

It must require a great deal of intelligence for humpbacks to memorize all of the complicated sounds, and the order of the sounds, in their song. Moreover, the song must be remembered for at least six months. Although all of the whales in a single group sing the same song, they sing it for only six months of the year. Each year, they change the song and add new parts to it,

so that it is quite different at the end of the six months than it was at the beginning. Yet six months later, when they return to the breeding grounds, they remember the song exactly as it was when they last sang it.

Humpbacks are baleen whales that eat krill and small fish. These clever animals trap food by swimming in a circle beneath a school of fish. As it circles, the whale blows bubbles from its blowhole. The bubbles rise in a column, creating a net of bubbles around the prey. Then the whale swims with open mouth up through the net, gathering in the trapped krill or fish. If the school is really large, two or more humpbacks work together to make a bubble trap.

Whales live in family groups and are truly loyal to one another. If one is injured or in distress, others come to its aid and stay beside it. They keep the injured one afloat by gently pushing it up with their noses or flukes, until it can swim on its own. Whales must breathe air. An injured whale would drown if not assisted.

Mother whales are especially devoted to their young and will not desert them even to save their own lives. One whale watcher reported seeing a female roll over on her back, drape her 150-pound calf across her chest, and pat it with her flipper. Young whales stay with their mothers for about six years. Each mother spends hours playing with her young and teaches it all the things it will need to know to survive.

Young whales are sometimes quite boisterous. They love to play and frolic with seaweed, but their favorite game is playing with their mothers' tail—sliding off one fluke, then the other. Sometimes one will get mischievous and cover its mother's blowhole or butt her in the side. Dr. Roger Payne, a well-known whale watcher, once saw a mother right whale roll onto her back just as her calf was about to ram her. She grabbed the youngster by clamping its tail to her side with her flipper. When the calf had settled down, she let it go.

Adult whales like to play with storms, leaping into the air and crashing into the waves. Dr. Payne saw right whales "sailing" during storms. The whales raised their tails straight up, at right angles to the wind. Then they let the wind blow them along. When they were blown into shallow water, the whales returned upwind, circled around, and took another sail, for all the world like otters sliding down a mud slide. They sometimes played this game for three or four hours.

Once a right whale lifted Dr. Payne's boat on its tail several times before gently setting it back down again.

Most whales are too large to live in captivity, but the United States Navy trained two beluga whales to attach harnesses to torpedoes that had been test-fired over very deep water in the Pacific. Some of the torpedoes sank without exploding. To recover these, the navy used the whales because they can dive much deeper than seals or dolphins. The whales learned very quickly.

Of course, some whales are smarter than others. The sperm whale is generally considered to be the most intelligent, because it has the largest brain of any known animal. Its brain weighs more than nineteen pounds. A human brain weighs a little more than three pounds. Dr. Jacques Cousteau, one of the world's authorities on whales, thinks that the small rocqual whale may be somewhat more highly developed and more clever than the 100-ton sperm whale.

Even the sperm whale's huge brain is not as large, in comparison to its body weight, as the dophin's brain. The bottlenosed dolphin's brain weighs nearly four pounds, and its body weighs only three hundred pounds. Its brain is about the same size as a human's brain and is just as advanced. It is more advanced than the brain of a chimpanzee or a gorilla.

Nonetheless, scientists cannot agree which is more intelligent, a chimpanzee or a dolphin. It is too difficult to compare these two very different kinds of animals. Everyone does agree however, that dolphins are highly intelligent animals. Dolphins are eager to cooperate, quickly grasp what is wanted, and learn complex tasks, as can be seen by the many tricks they perform in oceanariums and the chores they perform for humans. Dolphins were trained to carry tools and messages to workmen on the ocean floor when *Sealab II* was built. They were also enlisted to locate divers who got lost in the dark ocean waters.

Scientists at Florida International University are using dolphins to teach vocabulary to retarded children. These children learn much faster when they have a dolphin for a teacher. One child gave four times as many correct answers when a dolphin brought him pictures drawn on boards than when his mother gave them to him.

Dolphins never seem to forget what they have learned. One remembered a trick after ten years. They easily run mazes on the first trials, and free dolphins herd fish.

Dr. John C. Lilly, a neurologist, is one scientist who thinks these friendly, fun-loving animals are smarter than chimpanzees. Dr. Lilly knows more about dolphins than anyone, because he has studied them for over thirty years. He says that dolphins learn to do complicated tricks quicker than most apes, but he doesn't think circus tricks measure the animal's true ability. He thinks the only way to test a dolphin's intelligence is to communicate with it. To date, that is not possible, but Dr. Lilly is convinced that someday he will talk with a dolphin. He thinks that

any animal with such a huge brain and the ability to communicate vocally must have enough intelligence to learn human language.

Dolphins obviously understand commands, words, cues, and hand gestures. They are also very good at mimicking. One dolphin even learned to imitate a brush sound used for scrubbing its tank. Dr. Lilly decided to try to teach dolphins to speak English. He succeeded in teaching several captive dolphins to say things like: "I'm a good boy," " All right, let's go," "Stop it," and "Bye-bye." One could even count to ten. But there was no indication that the dolphins knew what they were saying. Human language is extemely difficult for a dolphin to produce. It is much too slow and too low in frequency.

Today Dr. Lilly is using the newest computer equipment available in an attempt to convert human speech into supersonic dolphin sounds and to translate the dolphin's noises into sounds that humans can hear. Dolphins make eighteen separate and distinct sound combinations, but much of their speech is in frequencies too high to be heard by the human ear. Once both dolphins and humans have learned a code of sixty-four sounds, Dr. Lilly expects to be able to carry on a conversation with the dolphins. He is sure dolphins are as eager to talk to us as we are to talk to them. Dr. Lilly is now working with free dolphins in their natural environment, the open sea.

No scientist who studies dolphins today doubts that these intelligent creatures communicate with one another, but the exact nature is not yet known. Scientists have taken tape recordings of dolphins "talking," and they have analyzed the tapes. They thought that perhaps they could learn to speak "dolphinese." The dolphins on the tapes took turns speaking, but there was no direct evidence that they were actually giving information to one another.

Dr. Jarvis Bastian, a psychologist at the University of California at Davis, decided to find out. He taught two bottle-nosed dolphins named Doris and Buzz a complicated game. First they were taught to press a lever with their snouts. Then he gave each dolphin two sets of levers. Next he taught the dolphins to press the right lever when they saw a flashing light and to press the left lever when they saw a steady light. They were given a fish every time they did this correctly, and they very quickly learned the difference between a flashing light and a steady light, and between the right lever and the left lever.

Now Dr. Bastian introduced a complication. When the light came on, Doris had to wait until Buzz pressed his lever. If she pressed hers first, she got no fish. After Buzz pressed his—*then* she was to press her lever. Finally Dr. Bastian placed a partition between the two dolphins. They could not see each other but could hear each other underwater. Only Doris could see the light. When Dr. Bastian turned on the light, Doris went to her lever and waited politely as she had been taught. When Buzz did not press his lever, she gave off a burst of whistles and clicks underwater. And somehow, Buzz, who could not see the light, knew which of his levers to push. Did Doris tell him? If he guessed, he was a shrewd guesser. He got it right every time!

With this evidence that dolphins do "talk" to one another, other scientists joined Dr. Lilly in attempting to communicate with dolphins. Since much of their language is too high for us to hear, other methods of communication have been tried.

Dr. Louis M. Herman, professor of psychology at the University of Hawaii, taught a dolphin a twelve-word sonic language and planned to teach her fifty more words. But former attendants released the dolphin into the open sea before he could complete the training.

William Langbauer is teaching two dolphins at Marineland of Florida to communicate, using black and white symbols similar to those that David Premack used with the chimpanzee, Sarah. The symbols are painted on metal rectangles that cling to a magnetic board.

Other scientists are trying to find out how much a dolphin knows. Biologist Earl Murchison learned that dolphins can tell the difference between shapes. He taught a female bottle-nosed dolphin to answer yes and no questions. If the answer was yes, the dolphin nudged a red ball. If the answer was no, she nudged a blue ball. Then Dr. Murchison lowered a shape into the water.

"Is anything out there?" he asked.

The dolphin nudged the red ball and got a fish for a correct answer.

"Is it cylindrical?" he asked.

Again the dolphin nudged the yes ball and received another fish.

Then Dr. Murchison lowered other cylinders of different shapes and sizes, and each time the dolphin answered correctly.

Then he lowered a length of angle iron and asked, "Is it a cylinder?"

The dolphin snorted and answered, "No."

Another dolphin could tell the difference between a ball that was 2½ inches in diameter and a ball that was 2¼ inches in diameter. When asked to pick the larger of two balls of the same size, it refused to try.

Dolphins seem to learn from one another. New animals learn a routine much faster if placed with one that is already experienced. A false killer whale once learned an entire show without ever receiving training or a reward. He only watched as his tank mates were being trained.

Scientists have not yet figured out a good way to test a dolphin's problem-solving ability, but many dolphins have shown that they are shrewd at solving their own problems. The dolphins in the oceanarium in San Francisco were taught to tidy up their pool. They received a piece of fish for each bit of trash they brought to their trainer. A dolphin named Mr. Spock was especially good at this and brought a steady stream of soggy scraps of paper. Finally his trainer learned that the dolphin had hidden a big brown bag in a corner of the pool and was tearing off one piece at a time!

Mr. Spock was training the trainer!

Once a sick dolphin at Marineland of Florida needed an antibiotic shot. Its attendant opened a gate so that it could go into a smaller tank where the veterinarian could give it the shot. Instead, the dolphin closed the gate and leaned against it. Its attendant managed to reopen the gate, but the dolphin must have realized it would get a shot if it went through. It closed the gate again. Now that was smart! Most animals would have retreated or run away, but this dolphin tried to solve the problem by doing something positive.

Free dolphins also learn from experience. Tuna often swim underneath dolphins, and dolphins are frequently caught in the fishermen's nets. A dolphin that has once been caught in a tuna net tries to be as quiet as possible whenever it sees another tuna boat approaching. It doesn't blow or spash. If the tuna boat finds it anyway, the dolphin tries to stay on the right side of the boat, since the nets are raised and lowered on the left side. If one does get caught, fishermen are required by law to let it go. The dolphin seems to know that it will be released. It stays patiently in the center of the net until the captain causes the net to bow. Then it races for the opening.

No animal is more playful than a dolphin. Sometimes a captive dolphin tries to teach a game to its trainer. If the trainer doesn't catch on, the dolphin expresses its displeasure by slapping the water with its tail and vocalizing in a loud manner or by hitting the trainer with its snout.

Dolphins can amuse themselves for hours with a floating feather or other object. They also love to tease. They pester sharks, turtles, pelicans, or anything else that lives in the same tank. Some grab things out of visitors' hands or pick up shells from the floor of their tank and throw them at passersby. Free dolphins romp with boats, leaping and splashing off the bow and taking a free ride in the wake.

These extremely social animals seem to enjoy human company. As far back as the ancient Greeks, there have been stories of dolphins who swam into sheltered coves and became friendly with children—even allowing them to ride on their backs. There has never been a report of a dolphin hurting a human—not even a killer whale, the largest of the dolphins.

Killer whales can snap a six-foot barracuda in two with one bite, but are tame and playful in captivity. One may nip or scratch a trainer if it is displeased, but none has ever injured anyone.

Killer whales are the smartest of the dolphins. They learn twice as fast as other dolphins and seem to understand everything their trainers say. Their brains are four times larger than a human's brain.

Shamu, a killer whale at Sea World in Florida, can perform 150 different acts. But he doesn't do them for a reward of fish. His reward might be a high-pitched whistle and a pat on the tongue, or an ice cube, or maybe a belly rub. Killer whales quickly become bored with the same routine day in and day out. Some dolphins invent new leaps and contortions to relieve the boredom of doing the same thing every time for the same fish reward. The trainers at Sea World learned that the best reward for this extremely intelligent animal was change, and occasionally a surprise.

The argument about whether a dolphin is more intelligent than a chimpanzee is unimportant. One dolphin is smarter than another. That can be measured.

Psychologists say that intelligence is the ability of an individual to successfully meet the demands of his environment. It may not be possible to compare accurately the intelligence of two entirely different kinds of animals, because each requires different types of intelligence to adapt to its own environment. Different environments require different kinds of behavior, and different kinds of behavior require different abilities. A necessary ability for one may be an excess for another. And an excess of any one ability may not be helpful in living a successful life. Good hearing is essential for a dolphin, but better hearing for a chimpanzee would not make it more intelligent. Similarly, while a good memory is necessary for intelligent behavior, an extraordinary memory is not necessarily useful in handling life's problems.

It is unnecessary to compare cetacean intelligence to human intelligence. Cetaceans know what they need to know for their survival, and that is all that matters. How intelligent do you suppose we seem to a dolphin? Surely many things we do must seem quite idiotic to this smart animal.

Testing
Your
OWNER'S
IQ

9

Testing Your Pet's Intelligence

Is your pet intelligent? Yes! But just how intelligent is hard to say. Although some people have tried to work out intelligence quotients for animals, these are even less accurate than those for humans. Intelligence is not an exact measurement like inches or pounds. An animal's intelligence cannot and should not be measured in the same way as a human's. For one thing, animals use different senses to explore their world. Raccoons use the sense of feel; dogs and cats depend mostly on the sense of smell; humans depend almost entirely on the sense of sight. Naturally, an animal that depends on smell will not do as well on a test requiring sight, but it might do better on a test requiring a sense of smell.

Generally, any time an animal changes its usual behavior and, by doing so, makes a distinct gain, it shows intelligence. The more quickly it changes its behavior, the more intelligent it is thought to be.

The following games and tests are intended to give you an opportunity to observe your pet's behavior under several different conditions. Think of them as something fun you can do with your pet—something both of you will enjoy. If you are lucky, you can also get a rough estimate of your animal's overall intellectual ability.

Select at least one game from each category. Choose the test or game best suited for your particular animal. For best results, perform tests just before feeding time. A hungry animal is easier to motivate. Don't try to do more than one test per day. For even better results, repeat each test three or four times on different days. Your pet may do poorly one day and extremely well the next. It may do much better on one kind of test than on another.

Carefully observe your pet's behavior and record its performance. Always give it a reward when it solves a problem. If a bite of food is a part of the test, allow the animal to eat it, when it correctly solves the problem.

Testing for Verbal Comprehension

The ability to understand and use language is considered to be a good indication of intelligence.

1. Make a list of words that you think your pet knows. For example: its name, words for food, specific commands you have taught it—"come," "sit," "down," and so forth. The longer the list, the smarter the animal is.
2. Select a command your pet usually responds to, but change your tone of voice when you speak it. For example, instead of saying "come!" sharply and emphatically, say it softly and drawn out or with an inflection.

   If your pet obeys the command, it understands the word. If it doesn't obey, it may not know the word and usually

reacts to the tone or gesture instead of the word. To further check this, give test number 3.

3. Make up a nonsense word such as *blop*. Use the same tone and gestures you usually do when giving a certain command. If your pet looks at you strangely, it is superior. An average dog obeys any command you usually give in that tone of voice. It reacts to tones and gestures, but does not understand words.

   Use this same procedure to test as many words as you reasonably can.

4. Go ten feet away from your resting pet. Call its name. If you get no response, try again. An average dog will wag its tail or in some way indicate it knows its name.

   Now try calling another name. How does your pet react? If it acted the same as when you called its own name, it does not know its name and reacts only to the sound of your voice.

   Next, call your pet as you usually do. An average pet comes when called, but does not respond to many other commands.

Attention Span and Curiosity

Your pet's attention span is a good measure of its intelligence. A dog that can concentrate on you for ten to fifteen seconds is sharper than one who loses interest after two or three seconds.

1. Make a sound that your animal has never heard before. If it cocks its head and displays an alert expression, this suggests good attention. If it gets up to investigate, it shows curiosity as well and should be rated superior.
2. Place an unfamiliar animal, such as a box turtle or a crab, on the ground in front of your dog. How does it react? An average dog will cock its ears, turn its head, sniff, and paw at the animal. A superior dog concentrates on the animal and refuses to be distracted. *It will not leave until the animal is taken away.*
3. Place some marbles or stones in a tin can. Hold the can behind your back. Stand six feet from your dog while it is lying on the floor (resting, but not sleeping). Rattle the can vigorously. An average dog cocks its ears, turns its head to one side, but does not investigate. A superior animal looks for the source of the noise.
4. Initiative and curiosity may be best observed in the everyday life of the animal, particularly young animals. For example, the first puppy or kitten in a litter to climb out of the box and begin investigating its surroundings is usually the smartest, as is the puppy or kitten that initiates play by nipping at the ears and tails of its littermates.

Concentration

Concentration is closely related to attention. Most of these tests work best with dogs, but with a little adjustment can be used with cats.

1. Place your dog on a leash and have someone hold it. Hide a small portion of its favorite food in each fist. (You need a bit of food in each hand so that the animal cannot simply sniff out the correct hand.) Hold your fists in front of you and show the dog the contents of one hand. Leave your hand open for a count of ten. Then close your hand and put both

hands behind your back. Leave them there while you count to thirty. Then hold both fists out in front again. Have the dog released as you call it. Encourage it to get the food. If it goes to the wrong hand (not the one you showed it), do not let it have the food. Repeat the next day. Does it do better on the second trial? An average dog will go to the correct hand in about thirty seconds on the second trial.

2. Place two empty cans upside down on the floor eighteen inches apart. Put a dog biscuit under one can. Then bring your dog in and have your helper hold the dog five feet away while you show the dog another biscuit. While it watches, place the biscuit under the second can. Count to thirty and have the dog released.

   If it goes directly to the second can and knocks it over, it is superior. An average cat or dog takes about a half minute to go to the correct can, but usually doesn't attempt to knock it over.

3. Place three plastic cups or bowls in a row eight inches apart on the floor. Put a bit of your pet's favorite food in the two outside cups and cover each with a small paper plate or cardboard disk. Bring your pet in and have someone hold it while you show it a morsel of the same food. Then place the food in the middle cup. Count to sixty and have the pet released.

   An animal that goes directly to the middle cup and retrieves the food is superior. An average animal goes to the correct cup before you can count to sixty, but it may go to the wrong cup first, then shift to the correct one.

4. Show your pet a bit of its favorite food. While it watches, hide the food under a towel. Observe what it does. An average animal will try several things to get the food—it paws, bites, sniffs—but it eventually retrieves the food (in about half a minute). Anything quicker than that is superior.

Does your pet do better on third and fourth trials? Does it learn from experience?

Common Sense and Good Judgment

Common sense and good judgment are important ingredients of intelligence.

1. Cut a breathing hole in the bottom of a paper bag. Slip the bag over your cat or dog's head. The bag should fit snugly, but not uncomfortably.

   An average pet will remove the bag within thirty seconds or before you count to sixty. Anything quicker is superior.
2. Throw a towel or small blanket over your pet's head. The quicker it removes the blanket, the smarter it is. An average dog frees itself within one minute.
3. Using only a single knot, loosely tie a two-foot-long piece of yarn or soft cord around your pet's muzzle. Don't put it tight enough to make it uncomfortable.

   An average pet removes the cord in half a minute.

   (Don't use this test on a dog that has had its mouth tied shut by the veterinarian when receiving shots. It will be conditioned to having its mouth tied shut and may not attempt to remove the cord.)

Reasoning and Insight

An animal's ability to solve problems is one of the best indications of its intelligence. The more intelligent the animal, the better it is at solving problems. Intelligent animals have the ability to try a new approach, if the first attempt fails. Unintelligent animals continue using the same approach time after time even after it is obvious this approach will not work. Unfortunately, some humans try to solve problems this same way. They have one-track minds and lack adaptability—the ability to try a different solution.

1. Let your pet smell a morsel of its favorite food. Then, while it watches, wrap the morsel loosely in a paper napkin or tissue. Drop the package on the floor about three feet from the animal (closer for a small animal).

   An average animal will get the package open in about

three to five minutes. Anything quicker should be considered superior.

2. Cut a slot along the bottom of each side of a large cardboard box. The slot should be big enough to admit one of your pet's paws, but not big enough to allow its head to go through. Let the animal watch you as you place a bit of its favorite food in the box and fasten the lid securely.

   A very superior animal quickly sizes up the situation and paws out the food. An average animal tries to get the food with its muzzle, but does not succeed, even after being shown how to do it.

3. Place a hungry cat or dog in a room that has a door that opens inward. Pull the door closed, but do not allow it to latch. Place the animal's favorite food just outside the door. If possible, have someone in the room observe the animal's behavior.

   An average cat or dog will push against the door, causing it to latch. A superior animal quickly opens the door. Cats pull it open with their claws; dogs open it with their snouts or a paw.

4. Place a four-foot barrier between the animal and its feeding dish. The barrier may be a window screen; a piece of fence; Plexiglas propped up with bricks, a chair, or a box; or cardboard with peek holes cut in it so that the animal can see the food but can't get through. The animal should be able to go around the ends of the barrier, but not over or under it. Have someone hold the pet while you put its favorite food in its dish. Make sure it sees you do this. Then have the animal released.

   A superior animal immediately goes around the barrier and gets the food. An average cat or dog goes to the barrier and makes an attempt to go through. It eventually wanders around the barrier and gets the food. A puppy or a bird may never find its way around.

   Does your pet improve with repeated trials?

5. For this test, you will need a large cardboard box (at least one foot tall and two feet wide). Tape shut the flaps on the top of the box and then cut the top loose on three sides, leaving it hinged to the box on the fourth side.

   Now, while your animal watches, place a small bit of its favorite food in the open box and encourage it to jump in and eat it. Do this three times. After it has eaten the last tidbit, put in one more piece of food and close the lid. What does your pet do?

   A superior animal lifts the lid and crawls into the box to obtain the food, although it may make several attempts before managing to lift the lid. An average pet will be able to obtain the food after being shown how.

Learning

Since even a worm can learn, it is the speed at which an animal learns that indicates its level of intelligence. These lessons should last no longer than twenty minutes per day. If your pet seems to tire before that time, stop and try again the next day. Expect to spend two or more weeks. Don't get angry if your pet doesn't cooperate. It may not like to show off.

1. Fasten a twenty-foot-long leash to your dog's collar. Place the dog about six feet from a tree or clothesline pole. Holding the leash, walk around the tree and stand about fourteen feet away from it (you will be about eight feet from the dog). Hold up a bone or dog biscuit and call your dog to you. An average dog strains for a long time, trying to get the bone before it realizes that it can get it by going around the tree. It needs to be shown fifteen or twenty times how to do it.

   A dog that goes back around the tree in order to reach the bone on the first attempt is a genius.
2. In a plastic cup or bowl, place a tidbit of food that your pet especially likes. Set it on the floor and let your pet eat it. Re-

peat several times. Then, while the pet watches, cover the cup (with tidbit inside) with a white paper plate or a cardboard disk. Let the animal discover that it can knock the lid off with its nose or paw. This will take a few minutes. Let it eat the tidbit. Repeat at least twenty times or until your pet knocks the lid off immediately, but not all on the same day. Then place two cups on the floor. Put a white plate on one and a black plate on the other. Always place the tidbit under the white plate. Repeat several times until your pet knows the food is always under only the white plate, and knocks off only that plate.

An average animal learns to get the tidbit by knocking off the plate, but doesn't learn that the tidbit is never under the black plate. A brilliant animal learns this in twenty or fewer lessons.

Memory

Memory has an important role in the intelligence of any animal.

1. While your dog watches, place a piece of dog biscuit in one of two boxes that are of different shapes or colors. Then take the dog for a ten-minute walk. When you return, permit the dog to go to the boxes. If he chooses the correct box, let him have the biscuit. Try again the next day. This time, walk for fifteen minutes. On the third day, walk twenty minutes. Can your pet still remember which box has the biscuit?

   An average dog remembers the correct box after a ten-minute walk, but not after fifteen minutes. Anything over twenty minutes is excellent.
2. Have someone hold your cat, but let it watch as you place its favorite food in its regular feeding dish. Let it sniff the food. Then set the dish on a box, chair, shelf, or some other unusual place, but one that the cat can get to. Make sure the cat sees where you put the food. Take the cat out of the room

and play with it for about ten minutes. Then take it back into the room where the food is.

An average cat goes to its usual feeding spot, sniffs, and eventually finds the food. A bright animal finds the food before you can count to sixty.

3. While someone holds your cat or dog, place its favorite toy or a small bit of its favorite food partway under a towel or cloth. Have the pet released and allow it to eat the morsel or play with the toy. Repeat two or three times. Then place the food or toy completely under the towel. A bright cat or dog will find it within a few seconds after being released.

   Next day, have a helper hold the animal ten feet from the towel. Place food under the towel and back off. Have the animal released.

   An average animal will get the food before you can count to 120. Anything faster is superior.

Special Tests for Special Animals

1. Play this game with a hamster, mouse, gerbil, or white rat. How quickly does it learn? Hold out a bit of favorite food—peanut or raisin—and call out the animal's name. Do this five or six times every day for four days. On the fifth day, do not offer food, but call its name exactly as you have been doing.

   If it is average, it will come to you when you call its name after two weeks of training. If it comes after the fifth day, it is extra bright.

2. This is similar to the first test, but this time hold the tidbit above the animal's head, just high enough so that it will have to stand on its hind legs to reach it. Say, "stand!" and call its name. Repeat until it stands. You may have to let it sniff the food first. Repeat four times each day until it will stand whenever you hold your hand over its head, even without the food.

An average small animal learns this lesson in about two weeks. Only a very bright one can learn it in one week.

3. Train goldfish to come when you tap on the side of the tank. Each time you feed the fish, tap on the bowl or aquarium before you sprinkle in the food. Sprinkle the food near the place you tapped, but give only a small amount. Then tap at the same spot every day, twice a day. Be sure to feed them every time you tap. After several weeks, the fish will come as soon as you tap. If your fish learn this with three weeks, you have very smart fish!

   As soon as you are sure the fish come for the tapping, feed the fish one day without tapping. Then tap the tank the next day. Do the fish come? Do they come after skipping two or three days? How long can they remember? Test to see. The longer their memory, the more intelligent they are.

Mazes

A maze is a series of T- or Y-shaped compartments or troughs that lead into each other with many blind alleys. An animal is placed in one end and observed as it makes its way to a reward of its favorite food or learns to avoid a mild electric shock.

A maze is a good way to discover how well an animal learns from experience. The first time it is placed in a maze, the animal explores it carefully, inspecting all passages. Eventually it comes to the end where it finds a bit of food. The next time it runs the maze, it goes down fewer blind alleys. Each time it is tested, it takes a more and more direct path and finishes in a shorter time.

When testing with mazes, conduct only one test each day.

1. Use a simple T-shaped maze to test an earthworm. You can construct one from plywood, Plexiglas, or cardboard, but three one-quart milk cartons will serve just as well. Cut one end and one side from each carton and tape them together to form a T. About midway down one arm of the T, place a

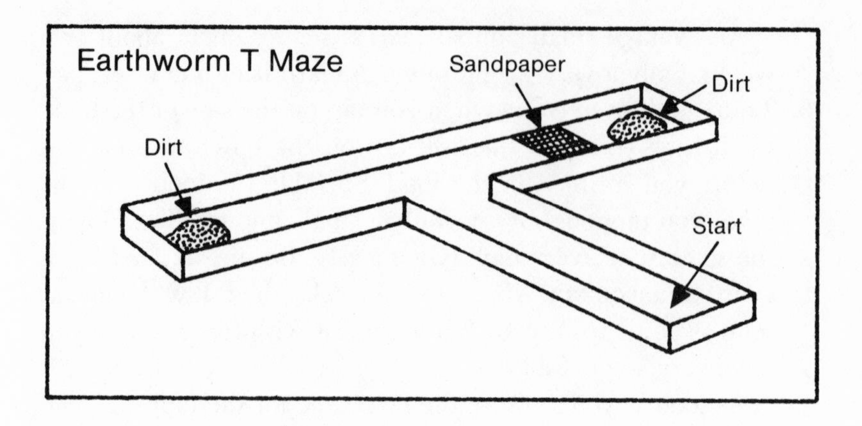

one-inch-wide strip of sandpaper across the arm. Place a small pile of moist dirt at the end of each arm. Then place your earthworm at the bottom of the T. (See diagram above.) If it turns down the arm containing the sandpaper, tap it gently on the end that is moving forward just as it crosses the sandpaper. If it goes down the other arm, allow it to burrow into the dirt for a few minutes, then return it to the bottom of the T. If your worm never goes down the arm with the sandpaper, move the sandpaper to the other side, and train it to go in the other direction. This test takes a lot of time and patience, but eventually the worm will learn not to turn down the arm with the sandpaper.

If the worm learns this in fifty trials, it is a pretty smart worm. One hundred trials is about average. After it has learned to avoid the arm with the sandpaper, stop for a few days. Then try the maze again. Did the worm remember and avoid the arm with the sandpaper?

2. Turtles are able to run slightly more complicated mazes than worms. At first, use no more than three T's connected together. These can be troughs like those of the earthworm, or if you want it more complicated, build a wandering path on stilts. Since the best reward for a turtle is a dip in water, have

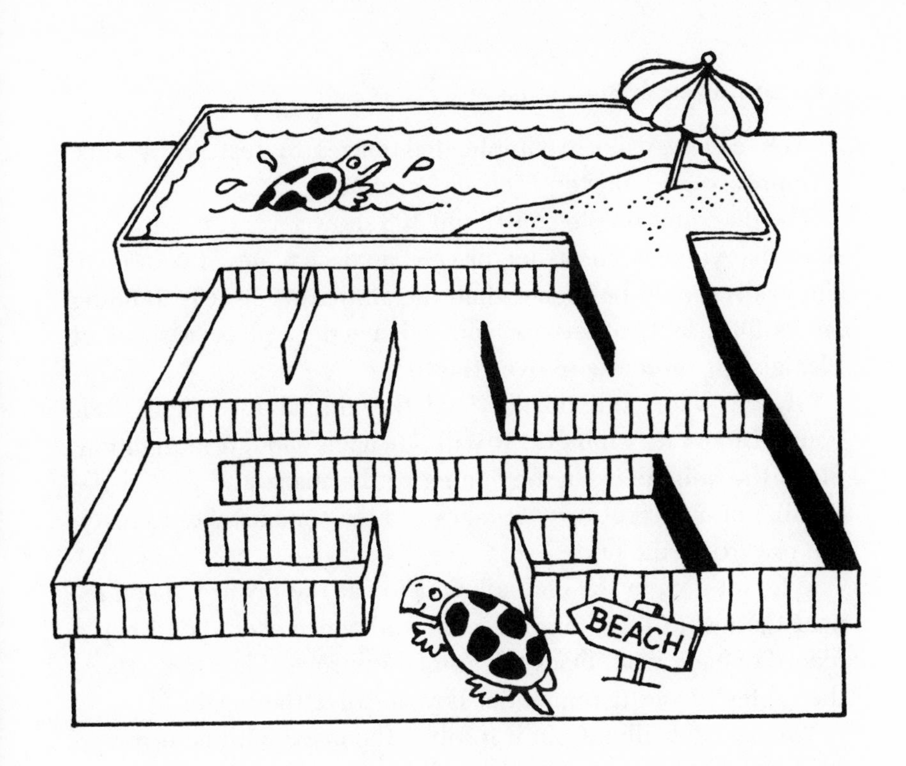

the last leg lead to a bowl of water. The turtle will learn that it has to stay on the path if it wants to reach the water. (See diagram below.)

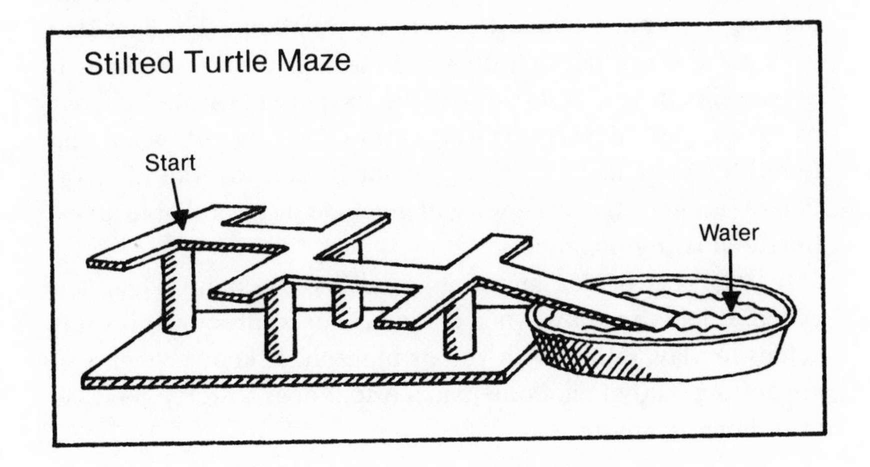

3. You can use more complicated mazes to test white rats, guinea pigs, hamsters, gerbils, or mice.

The diagrams on pages 107 and 108 show several possible designs that you can construct, or you can design one of your own. The walls should be higher than the animal when it is standing on its hind feet; otherwise you will need to place a sheet of Plexiglas or screen wire over the top.

Give it water but do not feed the animal for twenty-four hours. Unless it is hungry, it will not have enough motivation. Place the animal at the beginning of the maze and record the number of incorrect turns it takes and the time it takes to reach the reward at the end.

When it gets to the end, allow it to eat the reward. Then repeat the test at least ten times, but only once each day. Keep a record of each trial. Does the animal improve? Skip three days, then retest. Does it remember how to solve the maze?

You have a brilliant pet if it solves the maze with no errors in ten trials and remembers how to do it after three days. An average small mammal makes fewer incorrect turns with experience, and most can solve it after twenty trials.

Do not be upset if your pet does not do as well as you expected. Remember, these tests are not infallible. The fact that your pet did not do well does not mean it cannot. Perhaps it doesn't like to take tests. Maybe the tests are not suited to your particular pet. Maybe you were not relaxed enough when you tested the animal. Don't worry about it. Your overall observation of its everyday behavior will give you just as reliable an estimate of its intelligence.

A bright cat or dog knows its mealtime. It comes when it is called. It lets you know when it wants in or wants out. It invents games to play, either with you or by itself. It knows when you are getting ready to go someplace. And it does a pretty good job of training its master.

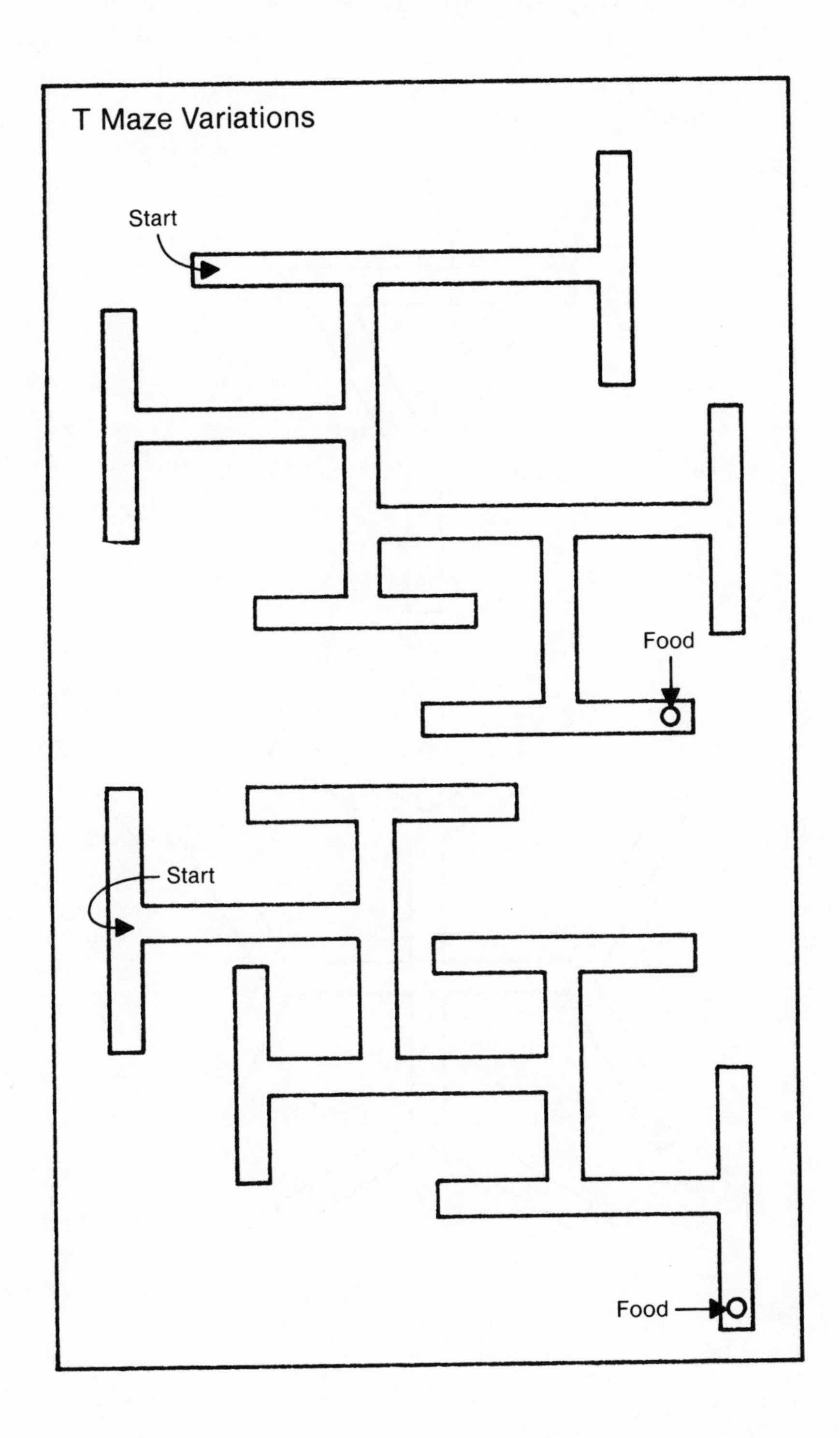
T Maze Variations
Start
Food
Start
Food

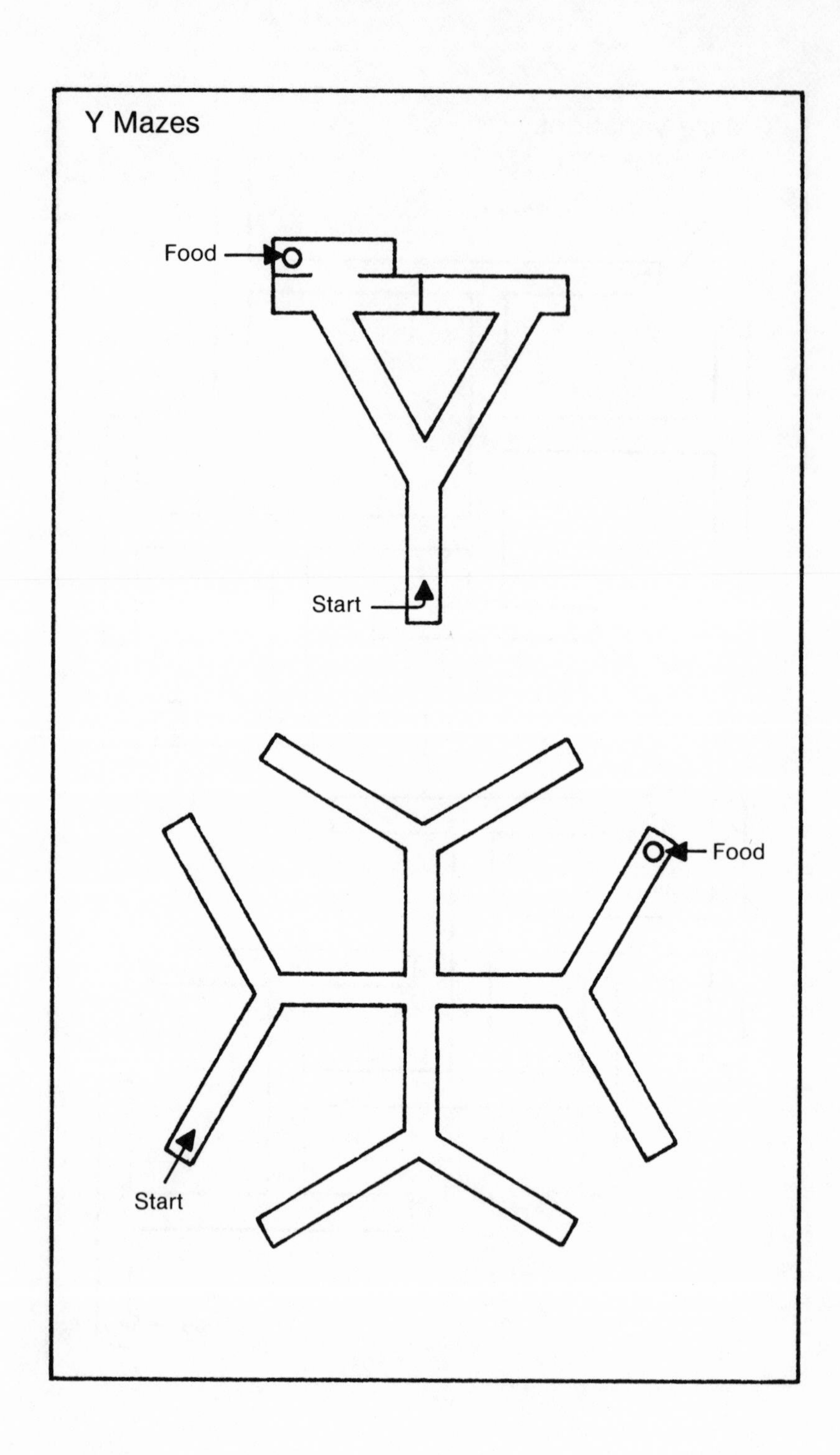
Y Mazes
Food
Start
Food
Start

Finally, even if your pet does seem to be only average, it is not any less lovable.

Personality, good manners, and dependability are qualities just as important for a happy and successful life as intelligence. Animals with only average intelligence often make better pets than extremely intelligent ones. With love, attention, and kindness, you can bring out all of the very best qualities of your pet.

INSTITUTE FOR ANIMAL STUDIES

10

Animal Studies and Human Learning

Scientists have learned many things from their studies of animal intelligence. Perhaps the most important is a better understanding of human intelligence. Many people have benefited as a result; many more will in the future, as scientists continue to apply the knowledge they have gained.

Scientists discovered that animals and humans learn in ways that are very much alike. This has helped them better understand human learning problems and mental retardation. As a result, many people with learning problems are leading happier lives today.

When scientists discovered that even a worm can learn, they searched for newer and better ways to teach severely mentally handicapped children. They experimented with methods used in teaching animals. Many handicapped children are now learning far more than anyone ever dreamed possible. Young retardates are taught to take care of themselves by being given varied routines and rewards for accomplishments, as was done with seals and killer whales. Already many have learned to feed themselves, go to the bathroom, and tie their shoes. Older children with a mental age of only one or two years are learning to "speak" for the first time, using computer keyboards and the Yerkish language designed for chimpanzees. Some are even learning to read with a simplified alphabet. This is exciting news.

Other researchers are having equally good results teaching autistic children to communicate with all three methods used with chimpanzees. These children have special mental problems that prevent them from communicating in a normal manner.

All children may eventually benefit from animal studies. It has been shown that animals in the laboratory learn to do tests better and remember them longer if they are prepared to learn what is being taught. It has been found that many children who once would have been considered slow learners can now be brought up to average by giving them sufficient stimulation and training at the preschool level. Studies show that children who have attended preschool learn better than those who did not. Similarly, children who are read to before starting school learn to read more easily, and they do better in math if they are taught to count at an early age. Better ways of providing early education are being explored.

Educators are also seeking more efficient methods to test children and ways to provide better environments full of challenges that stimulate curiosity, creativity, and problem-solving abilities.

Experiments show that a well-balanced diet is also important to learning. Ants that ate a good diet during their growing stages learned better than those that ate a poor diet. Similar experiments with children show that those who ate balanced diets rich in proteins and vitamins increased their ability to learn, too.

Scientists hope that their studies with animals will help prevent most of the problems that now create slow learners and will lead to improvements in the learning abilities of all children. Children of tomorrow may be brighter than those of today.

Further Reading

Books

Baky, John S., ed. *Humans and Animals.* New York: Wilson Company, 1980.

Berrill, Jacquelyn. *Wonders of How Animals Learn.* New York: Dodd Mead & Co., 1979.

Cohen, Daniel. *Intelligence: What Is It?* New York: E. P. Dutton, 1974.

Durrell, Gerald, *A Bevy of Beasts.* New York: Simon & Schuster, 1973.

Frings, Hubert and Mable. *Animal Communication.* Norman, Oklahoma: University of Oklahoma Press, 1964–1976.

Griffin, Donald R. *The Question of Animal Awareness.* New York: The Rockefeller University Press, 1976.

Holyer, Ernie. *The Southern Sea Otter.* Austin: Steck-Vaughn Co., 1975.

Lilly, John C. *Communication Between Man and Dolphin.* New York: Crown Publishers, 1978.

Lorenz, Konrad. *King Solomon's Ring.* New York: Time, Inc., 1962.

Morris, Desmond. *Animal Days.* New York: William Morrow, 1980.

Patterson, Francine, and Linden, Eugene. *The Education of Koko.* New York: Holt, Rinehart and Winston, 1981.

Shepard, Paul. *Thinking Animals: Animals and the Development of Human Intelligence.* New York: Viking Press, 1978.

Tinbergen, Niko. *Curious Naturalist.* New York: Doubleday, 1968.

Magazines

Battista, O. A. "Outwitted by Ants—and Their High IQ's." *Science Digest,* May 1978, pp. 64–66.

Burney, David A. "Life on the Cheetah Circuit." *Natural History,* May 1982, pp. 50–58.

Carter, Janis. "A Journey to Freedom." *Smithsonian,* April 1981, pp. 90–100.

Clark, Eugenie. "Sharks: Magnificent and Misunderstood." *National Geographic,* August 1981, pp. 138–186.

Ellis, Richard. "The Mammal Behind the Myths." *Science Digest,* January 1982, pp. 62–67.

Fossey, Dian. "Making Friends with Mountain Gorillas." *National Geographic,* January 1970, pp. 48–67.

Galdikas, Biruté. "Living with the Great Orange Apes." *National Geographic,* June 1980, pp. 830–853.

Goodall, Jane. "My Life Among Wild Chimpanzees." *National Geographic,* August 1963, pp. 272–308.

Menzel, Randolf, and Erber, Jochen. "Learning and Memory in Bees." *Scientific American,* July 1978, pp. 102–110.

Parfit, Michael. "Are Dolphins Trying to Say Something or Is It All Much Ado About Nothing?" *Smithsonian,* October 1980, pp. 73–80.

Payne, Roger, and Nicklin, Flip. "New Light on the Singing Whales." *National Geographic,* April 1982, pp. 463–476.

Premack, David. "The Education of S*A*R*A*H: A Chimp Learns the Language." *Psychology Today,* September 1970, pp. 55–58.

Rensch, B. "The Intelligence of Elephants." *Scientific American,* February 1957, pp. 44–49.

Würsig, Bernd. "Dolphins." *Scientific American,* March 1979, pp. 136–148.

Index

About the Author

Helen Roney Sattler says: "The nature of intelligence has always fascinated me. I am particularly interested in the incredible abilities of the so-called dumb animals and want to share this fascination with children. I believe that children can better understand the complicated and controversial nature of human intelligence by learning about the intellectual capabilities of animals." Mrs. Sattler, who lives in Bartlesville, Oklahoma, has taught elementary school and has been a children's librarian in addition to writing and illustrating many books for young people.

About the Illustrator

Giulio Maestro has illustrated more than seventy books and has written several riddle books. He grew up in New York City and now lives in Madison, Connecticut.

4482